Singer Island

By

Wanda James

This book is a work of fiction. Places, events, and situations in this story are purely fictional. Any resemblance to actual persons, living or dead, is coincidental.

ISBN: 1-4033-1711-9

This book is printed on acid free paper.

1st Books - rev. 04/20/02

I would like to dedicate this book to my grandmother who I miss very much. Her storytelling is what inspired me to become a writer. Rosa E. Harris had a gift for weaving tales of excitement and adventure. I only hope I do justice to my own creations.

CHAPTER ONE

Priscilla stood looking at the house. It had been eighteen years since she left with Mary. She never expected to be back here again. Priscilla would rather leave well enough alone. She felt blessed to be able to get off the wretched island the first time. Now here she was right back where it all started.

Priscilla had watched Charles, her brother, grow into a man and marry. Mary was their only child. Charles loved his wife dearly, he was severely grieved when she died in childbirth. Charles was never the same, he left his baby daughter with his loving sister. Charles left to try to start his life over.

But that never happened. He was a lonely man, suffering deep within himself. Priscilla hardly heard from her brother. When she did, he rarely mentioned Mary. Priscilla knew Mary reminded Charles of his late wife Elizabeth and his loss.

Mary was a happy and well-adjusted child; she looked on her aunt as one would a mother. Priscilla was the only parent she ever knew. Priscilla took care of all of Mary's needs. She wouldn't hear of a nanny. Mary had lost a father and a mother, Priscilla couldn't stand the thought of a stranger tending to Mary's needs. Mary was as devoted to Priscilla as Priscilla was to her.

As the years passed, Mary grew into a beautiful and graceful young lady. She seldom went far from home. Priscilla thought it was time she took a trip to Savannah, Georgia to visit a cousin there. No respectable young woman traveled alone in those days, so Priscilla would accompany her on her journey. Mary saw her cousins only on holidays. She was very excited about the trip. Priscilla ordered a new wardrobe made for her and Mary.

Travel arrangements were made, they would set sail for Savannah in three days. But before they sailed, a letter came for Mary. It told her of an inheritance from her father. Over the years, she often wondered what sort of man he was. Aunt Priscilla wouldn't tell her very much of her father's life. She only knew that he went away when her mother died and left her with his sister.

The letter told of an island her father had owned. It was called Singer Island, where he lived in a cottage until his death. Pris didn't want Mary going to the Island because of the mysterious things that happened there during her childhood. Mary told Pris she needed to go to her father's Island. She needed to know about this man that was her father.

Pris and Mary boarded the boat headed to Savannah. The journey to Savannah was pleasant. The ocean was calm, and the sun sparkled like diamonds on the water. Mary was on deck enjoying the ocean breeze, as well as the sunshine. This was a treat for her.

As Mary stood by the railing, her mind wondered back to the letter from her father. Oh why did he wait so long to get in touch with me? I could have gotten to know him before he died. Fate robbed her of both parents. Priscilla was wonderful to her though. Mary couldn't have asked for a better parent.

Priscilla was in their cabin unpacking. They would be on board for nine or ten days. Maybe longer, if the weather turned ugly. Mary for one hoped it stayed calm. She didn't look forward to rough water. Mary heard the stories about sea sickness before leaving home.

Mary would just as soon have a pleasant trip she cared to remember. Mary explored every inch of the boat. It fascinated her. How could something so big stay afloat? There were quite a few people aboard headed somewhere. Most were late travelers returning home from the Thanksgiving holiday.

Mary met a young man from Savannah, Georgia. Henry Collins was returning home from a holiday with his grandparents in St. Augustine, Florida.

Henry joined Mary and her aunt for their first dinner on board that night. Mary got a little sunburn during the day. Her face was pink from a mixture of sun and wind. Priscilla told her to use face cream to help with the burning.

"Mary, on the ocean you have to be more careful. There are no trees out here to shade you. Next time, remember to come in out of the sun sooner."

Mary didn't mind much. She enjoyed every minute of her day. Henry was a good conversationalist. Priscilla was taken with him immediately. Henry was a very well mannered and educated young man. Pris could tell he was taken with Mary. At least she would have someone on board to have fun with during the trip.

"Mary, would you like to go out on deck and watch the moon and stars? They are quite beautiful tonight."

"Henry, that would be nice. I'm too excited to sleep." They strolled on deck for awhile. Mary told Henry about the trip to her cousins in Savannah.

"How long will you be in Savannah before going home?"

"We will be in Savannah for two weeks. Then, we will journey to my father's island. I received a letter before we left, from my father. He left me his island. I've never been there, except when I was born. Pris took me to Monet, after my mother died, and raised me."

"I am sorry Mary. That is very sad."

"I never got to know either of my parents. My father left and never came back for me." They continued walking around the deck enjoying the night.

"Mary, why are you going to this place now? As I said, I've never been there."

"He must want me to see the island for he sent me the deed."

This bothered Henry, he couldn't explain it, but something didn't feel right about her receiving a letter after so many years.

"Mary, I will visit you in a few weeks, with your permission. I have some business to attend to in Pineda. It would be nice to come across to Singer Island to see you."

"Henry you're welcome to visit anytime." The days passed quickly on the Santa Rosa for Henry and Mary. Priscilla pretty much stayed in. The ocean air didn't agree with her arthritis. Pris really suffered through the winter months. Even though the winters here were hardly ever below sixty-eight or seventy degrees. Pris still preferred summer to winter any day. It was no fun getting old. Her mind didn't feel old at all, just her body. Tonight was the last night out. Tomorrow they would dock in Savannah. Pris was glad. She was starting to get cabin fever when the boat docked at eleven that morning. Everything was packed and ready to be moved to Edwards home. Mary said her farewells to Henry. Henry promised a visit very soon.

Henry stood on the dock and watched Mary leave with her family. She was so beautiful. Priscilla and Mary were met by her cousin Edward at the docks. Edward took Mary and Priscilla to his home on River Street, in the wealthiest section of town. There was easy access to the river to transport merchandise.

As they arrived, the house was buzzing with activity, getting things ready for their stay. Mary's cousins planned several balls in

Mary's honor on her stay here in Georgia. Mary loved the excitement, she led a rather sheltered life with Priscilla. Priscilla was as excited as Mary. Many years had passed since Pris was socially involved. She realized she missed it. The sacrifice was worth it when she looked at Mary.

After Mary and Priscilla were settled in their rooms, Cynthia came to tell them lunch was ready. Cynthia was the youngest of four daughters. There was Abigail, who was nineteen, Andorra, who was seventeen, Josephine, who was fifteen, and Cynthia, who just turned thirteen.

Mary loved her cousins. When they were together, they had lots of fun. The house was full of activity with the girls getting fitted for their gowns by Mrs. Ferguson the seamstress. The materials were exquisite. Silks, satins and chiffon were the choices for evening attire.

Abigail wore a yellow chiffon dress with a ribbon sash. It looked gorgeous with her dark hair and her green eyes. Andorra's gown was made of satin, teal in color with a long flowing train. Andorra's hair color was the deepest black, almost blue. Her eyes were green with yellow flecks.

Josephine was completely different. Her hair was the color of honey. Her eyes were blue. Josephine chose a silk gown with a low neckline and puffed sleeves, slender at the waist with a flowing train. It was powder blue.

Cynthia chose a chiffon dress with bows in the back. She chose a lilac color. She had auburn hair and dark brown eyes. Mary was impressed with their choices.

Mary decided on a satin gown, the color of spun gold, with a slender waistline. The material felt marvelous. It was so soft.

Mary would pick one more. The last dress was chiffon. It fit tight across the bodice and flowed straight to the floor. Mary loved its color, light green. This concluded her attire for the parties she would attend while in Savannah. She really didn't need clothes like this where she was going.

Mary and her family attended a party that evening. It was hosted by the Frederick family. They were new to Savannah. The house was buzzing. Mrs. Frederick met her guest at the door.

Mary was intrigued with the various gowns the women wore. They were so beautiful. The music consisted of waltzes, and foxtrots. Priscilla fit in perfectly. It was as though she did this every day.

Mary's cousins were on the dance floor with their gentleman friends. Mary wished that Henry were present. Mary was shy around people she didn't know. After an hour of dancing, Mrs. Frederick called to everyone that dinner would be served in the main dinning room in about fifteen minutes.

Mary found Pris and they went into the dinning room together. The meal was fit for a king! Fondue, Pheasant under glass with asparagus almandine and a mixture of broiled shrimp, tomatoes, rice, peppers and onions. The deserts were divine! Chocolate soufflé, chocolate cake, strawberry shortcake, pecan pie, and sweet potato pie. Mary was in heaven.

After dinner everyone returned to the dance floor. Mary mingled with the guest. It was a night she would not soon forget. It was after one in the morning before the party ended. Mary was tired, even though she was excited. After getting ready for bed, Mary and Josephine sat talking for awhile. The days ahead would be just as much fun.

Several parties had been planned. Edward had accepted everyone's invitation's for his cousins. He wanted them to enjoy the stay here. Edward knew they lived a simple, quiet life.

Edward would really have liked Priscilla and Mary to move to Savannah. Mary would have opportunities here unavailable in Monet. Savannah was well known for social gatherings. A lot of influential people attended the parties. People came here from the north in the winter for the warm climate. Most of the houses belonged to people from the north.

Mary finally fell asleep around two in the morning. She never knew life could be so busy. Mary was enjoying it, but wouldn't want to do this everyday. Mary liked the tranquil life of Monet.

The sun was shinning bright when Mary awoke. She could hear the hustle and bustle downstairs. Mary wondered if Pris was up. She got out of bed looked out her window to the street below. People were already up and busy. Mary dressed in a light pink pinafore. Everything was ready for her second party tonight. This would be in the home of Henry Ford. Another prominent man of Savannah and St. Simons Island, Georgia.

Mary's cousins were in the dinning room when she came down. Mary was hungry. She found bacon, sausage, pancakes, eggs, gravy, and biscuits. She got a plate from the sideboard and sampled a little of everything. Mary covered her pancake with strawberry jam. She sat chatting with her cousins as she ate. Andorra was meeting her beau for lunch.

Josephine was reading for Mrs. Ford. Mr. Ford's mother enjoyed her visits. Abigail planned to help her mother polish the silver. Cynthia was chattering a mile a minute. She attached herself to Mary.

Mary didn't mind, she often wished she had a sister to share secrets with. Pris tried to be a friend and companion to Mary, but she was older. Cynthia was very informative about all the parties. Who would attend, what the homes were like. Who was more influential in the community. By the end of the day, Mary felt like she knew all of the hosts very well. Mary dressed in her blue gown that was made of silk. The skirt was full and when she twirled it made a swooshing noise. She brought her hair up on top of her head, leaving curl's hanging from each side of her face. Mary looked exquisite.

Pris was dressed in a black flowing gown with fur around the cuffs of the sleeves. She looked magnificent. It made her look ten years younger. Maybe this life style would be better for Pris. Mary couldn't remember seeing Pris so alive.

The party started around eight. The evening was cool and clear. The house was all lit up. People were beginning to arrive. Mary stayed pretty close to her cousins. She was introduced to everyone her cousin's knew. A lot of people were at last night's party. Mary liked Mrs. Ford. Her smile was genuine.

Mary danced until she thought her feet would drop off. She didn't care she would always cherish the memories. Pris went back to Edward's around midnight. Mary was still going strong. She wanted to pack every moment as full as possible.

Mary tried all the foods in moderation. Thank goodness she never put on weight. Around two in the morning, Mary was dead on her feet. She needed to go home and get in bed.

Two thirty in the morning Mary was brushing her hair getting ready for bed. She fell asleep and dreamed of ballrooms filled with dancing people.

By eight, Mary was up and ready for the day. She wanted to see Savannah. Cynthia would take her around today so she could see the town. Mary's next party was planned for her last night in Savannah. Tonight it would just be family. The days passed quickly.

It was the last night before their departure to the Island. The party took place around seven. The Gilmore's were new to Savannah. They fit right in. Old money fits in anywhere, Mary was finding out.

Mary would wear the chiffon dress to the last party. It was pale green. The seamstress had created a masterpiece. It was the most comfortable dress Mary ever wore. Mary was a little sad that her two weeks in Savannah were coming to an end. She never once saw Henry at any of the gatherings. Mary knew they were wealthy. Why were they not at the parties? Maybe they didn't like parties.

Mary enjoyed the last party with all her cousins gathered around her. Over the past two weeks they had bonded together. She would miss them. Tonight she wouldn't stay out so late. She was due to catch a boat at ten. Mary needed to pack a few more things before then.

The last garment was packed and her trunks were sitting by the door ready to go. For now, Mary needed some sleep. As soon as her head hit the pillow she was sound asleep. She hated to leave but with the adventure of her expedition to the Island she was happy again.

When they arrived at the docks, everyone was teary eyed not wanting the time to end. They all loved Mary and Pris. They bid their farewells and were off on another journey of the unknown.

CHAPTER TWO

Pris felt a little apprehensive about this trip. She remembered the things that went on their in her childhood. But Mary could not be stopped. It was an obsession with her at this point.

Mary and Pris boarded the Angelina that morning headed for Pineda, Florida. From there, they would catch a smaller boat to Singer Island. The trip would take about six days. Both needed that time to catch up on some much needed rest. The parties were great, but if one were not used to that life style, it could be a bit much.

Mary would write her cousins a thank you note for the lovely holiday. The first night on the Angelina was filled with music in the galley. Mary and Pris both quite enjoyed their meal along with the soothing music. An early night was planned. Both were exhausted.

It was a rather chilly night on the Angelina. It was late November, the nights were much cooler than the days.

The beds were turned down in their cabins. Hot water bottles wrapped in towels were placed under the covers at the foot of the bed. Mary was delighted. She was cold from being outside for about half an hour looking at the water. Being out on the ocean was marvelous. After crawling into bed, the splashing of the water against the boat rocked her to sleep.

Mary slept about seven hours before she awoke. The sun wasn't up yet. She lay listening to the sounds of the water and the crew working. Mary didn't bother to get up for another couple hours.

Pris woke up with a craving for sausage and pancakes with lots of jam. This was not her usual breakfast. Something about the salt air made her hungry. Mary was hungry by the time she got up and dressed. She needed coffee. Mostly to warm her up. It was damp today. Mary hoped Pris wouldn't suffer with her arthritis too bad today.

Mary would keep hot water bottles for her to curl up with to keep her bones warm. Pris never complained. No need worrying Mary. Each enjoyed her breakfast. Mary had eggs benedict and biscuits with jam and coffee.

After breakfast, they returned to the cabin to talk about the past two weeks in Savannah.

"Pris I've never seen you so alive. Maybe we should move to Savannah. You could stay more active socially."

"No, Mary, I'm too old. That's nice for awhile, but it's not a life style for me anymore."

"Well, if it were, I would consider the move for you."

"That's sweet, Mary, but I'm happy in Monet. We've lived there eighteen years. That's home to me."

As the days passed Mary and Priscilla were revived. About all you can do on a boat is eat and rest. An occasional stroll around the deck. Mary enjoyed Priscilla's company. She never got bored when she was with Pris.

Priscilla was a very knowledgeable woman. Over the years she tutored Mary in French, Spanish, history, as well as, how to care for a home.

On the fifth night aboard, the captain joined them for their final meal aboard. He was very pleasant to be with.

Mary was eager to land at Pineda and find someone to take them to Singer Island. Pris still tried to convince Mary to abandon this trip one last time. She hoped the house wasn't livable. Then they could turn around and leave. Pris would see. She had not returned there for eighteen years.

On arrival at Pineda, Mary found someone willing to take them over. The captain of the shrimp boat agreed to check on them every three or four days. The house was just as Pris had remembered. For it to have sat for years unattended it was in good shape.

On her first night on the Island, Mary went for a stroll on the beach. She felt uneasy while walking the remote beach, but she knew no one was here but her and her aunt. Mary returned to the house just before dusk. Pris was sitting in the parlor waiting for her return. Mary told Pris of the uneasy feeling she felt while strolling along the beach. Pris asked Mary to promise not to be out alone on the Island. Mary asked why.

Pris told her, "You don't know this Island and you could get lost."

Mary rose to pour a cup of tea, "Will you join me Aunt Pris?"

"No, dear it's been a long day for an old woman. I think I will retire for the evening. Promise to lock all the doors and windows before you go to bed."

Mary laughed and told her aunt that she worried too much. "But if it will make you feel better, I promise I'll lock up." Mary sat a while drinking her tea and thought maybe it would be a good idea to have some servants around. After all, they were two helpless women.

Mary's sleep was very restless that night, but in spite of that fact she was up very early. Pris was already in the kitchen making coffee when Mary strolled in lazily. Mary looked as if she hadn't slept at all. Mary kissed her aunt good morning and sat down with her coffee.

"Aunt Pris, I've decided maybe we shouldn't be here alone, so we'll go to the mainland for supplies and hire some servants." Pris hoped after arriving, Mary would want to leave, but that didn't seem to be the case. Pris told Mary if they were staying that would be a splendid idea.

Mary and Pris arrived in Monet around ten a.m. and were asking around about servants. The man at the butcher shop told her of an old woman across town who would more than likely work for her. "But, Miss Windsor, don't be surprised if no one will step foot on that wretched island." He would not tell Mary why. Mary thanked him and asked if she could pick up her bundles on the way back to the docks. The butcher assured her it would be fine, so Mary got directions to Mrs. Bunt's house.

When Mary arrived, Mrs. Bunt welcomed her. Mrs. Bunt told Mary she knew her family long ago. Mary hired Mrs. Bunt and told her to meet her at Pineda Bluff within the hour. Mary went back and picked up her supplies and arrived at the docks at one.

Mrs. Bunt arrived shortly after. Mary was on her way back to Singer Island. She made arrangements with a fisherman to deliver supplies. He told her he would leave them at the dock, because he would not step foot on the island. She said to him it was a beautiful island and no harm would come to him. He told Mary the island was evil. "There have been a lot of people come to this island and never been heard of again."

Mrs. Bunt told the old man, "Don't frighten the dear girl with your fisherman's tales." Pris listened quietly, for she too knew of the horrors of Singer Island. "If only I can get Mary away from here before it is too late," she thought.

CHAPTER THREE

They arrived at the island around two. Each was burdened down with supplies to be carried to the house. Everyone was exhausted from the boat ride and carrying supplies to the house, so they agreed to take a short nap.

Mary went to her room, it was very cool there, even though it was very hot outside. She took a blanket from the closet and lay down on the bed to wonder about the Island her father left her. She drifted off to sleep only to be awakened with a fright around four in the afternoon. She felt as though someone was in the room with her, but she saw no one. Whatever awakened her, frightened her.

She got up, splashed water on her face, fixed her hair and went down stairs. She just wanted to be near someone.

Aunt Priscilla was in the kitchen with Mrs. Bunt. When Mary went down, they were talking like old friends. Pris noticed Mary as she entered, she looked a little pale. Mary told Pris of her fright, but brushed it off as just being in a strange place. Pris begged her to abandon the idea of staying here, but Mary wouldn't hear of it. In the back of Priscilla's mind she knew it was only a matter of time before it all happened again as it had so many years ago.

Mary's mother, Beth, was brought here as a young bride. After her marriage to Charles, strange things began to happen. Charles was certain it was only that she was young and, being isolated on the Island, her imagination got the best of her. Beth started walking the floors at night. She confided to Pris something was keeping her awake, and she was afraid of whatever it was in the dark that she could not see. She told Pris her room became unbearably cold at night. She felt as if someone was there watching her.

Pris told Charles of there conversation. He thought it was from being on the Island with nothing to do. Charles agreed to spend more time with Beth and planned a trip to the Georgia Coast.

Beth was thrilled about the trip and Pris never heard anything else about the strange things that went on in Beth's room at night. Charles and Beth departed on a Thursday. While they were gone, Beth became pregnant with Mary. After a month Charles told Beth it was time to return home. Beth felt fine since they left the Island and with the excitement of a baby, Beth begged Charles not to return to the

Island yet. But Charles told her he needed to get back and take care of business. "I have neglected work since our trip." Charles assured Beth everything would be different when they got home, but Beth was terrified, not just for herself now, but for her unborn child.

They returned to the Island one April night, just around midnight. Beth was never the same, she began to look pale, but everyone thought it was from her pregnancy. She wouldn't leave the house at all, so Charles sent for a Doctor to come over from Pineda to care for her. They were very concerned for the unborn child. They didn't know if Beth would try to do away with herself. At night she roamed the house. She said someone was calling her name, but she never found anyone. No one else heard these things. They just looked at her with pity. She was so young to be in this state of mind.

Charles was beside himself with worry. He couldn't stand to see his Beth like this. He worried the child was too much, and felt a guilt he couldn't live with for bringing her back to the place she was so afraid of. On November 23, 1783, Mary was born. Beth was so weak from childbirth that a week later she died. Charles was immensely grief stricken over the loss of his young wife. Beth was buried in the family cemetery two days later. Charles thought, "If I had only listened and not come back here, Beth would be alive." Charles closed the house and asked Pris to take Mary until he could recover.

Pris and Mary went to a little town on the coast of Florida. Pris owned a house there, where she and Mary spent the next eighteen years. Now Pris was back on the Island with Mary. She would not stand by and watch it all happen with Mary, as she did with Beth. She would find a way to protect Mary from whatever plagued her family.

Mary told Pris, "If father did not want me on the Island, he would have left it to someone else." There was nothing Pris could do except watch out for Mary's well being.

Dinner was finished and the table cleared when Mary told Pris she was going for a walk. Pris warned Mary not too go far, because it would be dark soon. Mary strolled down toward the dock thinking about her father's island. She was caught up in thought when she heard a scream that made the hair on the nape of her neck stand on end. She turned to go back to the cottage. Suddenly, her path was crossed by something or someone. She could see a lot of hair and thought it was an animal, but it was walking on two legs, instead of four.

She was afraid to breath. The creature just looked at her and turned and ran away. Mary was never so frightened in all her life. The light was dim. She thought it might be her imagination, perhaps it was just a wild animal of some kind. Mary got to the house and found Pris in the parlor. She told Pris what she thought she saw, "but I can't be sure." Pris made Mary promise not to go out alone again.

That night Mary couldn't sleep, her room was unbearably cold. She couldn't figure it out, the rest of the house was hot. Mary went downstairs hoping not to wake Pris or Mrs. Bunt. She went out the side door of the parlor to the patio. Mary was thinking how good a swim would be. She walked down the path to the beach, stripped off down to her underwear and walked into the refreshing waves. She swam in the moonlight until she was exhausted.

When she came out of the water, the strangest feeling came over her that something was watching her. She called out, "Is anyone there?" All her fears of the evening returned. She picked up her clothes and hurried home.

Mary let herself back in through the parlor and headed for her room to get some dry clothes. The room was freezing. She dressed quickly and crawled into bed. She fell asleep immediately and dreamed someone was chasing her along the beach. Mary couldn't see who or what it was, but she was scared.

Pris was up a long time before Mary arose the next morning. Previously, Mary was up early, but since coming to this wretched island, she often slept late. Mary was a happy carefree young woman, but lately she was becoming quiet and withdrawn. Mrs. Bunt was cooking breakfast when Pris came down and asked Mrs. Bunt to keep something warm for Mary. "Mrs. Bunt, did you hear anyone rambling around last night?"

Mrs. Bunt assured her she heard nothing. "I sleep very soundly, I was blessed with that ability."

"When we retire tonight, we'll check all the doors and windows to make sure they're locked."

When Mary came down stairs, it was around eleven. Mary never slept late and Pris asked Mary if she was ill. "No, Pris, I couldn't get to sleep again. I went for a swim and came back and fell into a troubled sleep."

"Mary, you promised not to go out after dark."

"I know, but it was so beautiful. The moon was full and the water was warm. I couldn't sleep, my room was so cold."

"You need to move out of that room, it's eerie."

"I feel drawn to that room."

"You never complained of having trouble sleeping until we came here. I just worry, you're all I have and I love you. Mrs. Bunt, will you build a fire in Mary's room this evening, maybe it will knock the chill out. I wish we could sell this island and go home."

"Pris, it's beautiful and I want to stay, for a while at least."

"If you only knew the heartache that happened here."

"Pris, why don't you tell me."

"It happened a long time ago and it's best forgotten."

Mary would not push Pris for now, but one day she would know. After breakfast, Mary told Pris she was going down on the beach. "Be careful, Mary, and don't stay too long."

Looking around in the light of day, Mary couldn't believe she had been frightened last night. Things looked different in the light of day. I'll just forget it and chalk it up to a run away imagination. Mary wandered along the beach and spotted a lighthouse near the end of the island. She walked toward it and thought of all the ships it must have helped to avoid running aground. The light house was in need of repair, so she climbed the stairs with caution. When she did, she saw an old building on the other side of the island. She promised herself she would explore it later. But now she was determined to make it to the house fast, a storm was coming.

Storms brew up fast along the coast. By the time Mary made it home, rain was coming down hard. She was soaked to the bone. Pris was in the parlor with a fire going. Pris told Mary to run up and change, "before you catch a cold." In the upstairs hall, Mary thought she caught a glimpse of someone. But she knew Pris and Mrs. Bunt were downstairs. She shrugged it off as poor lighting and went into her room. Even with a fire in her room, it was still cold. She dressed hurriedly and returned to the parlor.

Pris made hot tea for her. She sat down and held it between both hands. It was warming her nicely. Pris asked Mary, "Where were you tonight?"

Mary told Pris of the lighthouse she found on the end of the island. "I climbed to the top and looked around. You can see the whole island up there. I saw a cabin on the other side, but before I could explore further the storm approached, forcing me to hurry home. I shall explore it tomorrow."

Pris remembered the house, it was the stableman's house. "There used to be old buildings around the island for the hired help. I would have imagined that they were all fallen down by now."

"Pris why did father close the house?"

"Well, Beth died and your Father couldn't stand the memories. He closed it and you and I moved to Monet."

"How did my mother die?"

"Mary she was very weak from your birth, it was too much of a strain on her."

"How long did you know her?"

"About two years or longer."

"Was she pretty?"

"Oh yes, Mary she looked just like you. She loved your father dearly. And Charles was very much in love with her. So you see why Charles couldn't stay here where her memory was still so much alive. He said he could see her everywhere. It tore him apart."

Mrs. Bunt entered the parlor and told them dinner was ready. After dinner, Mary asked Pris if she would play whist. They played three hands and Mary asked Pris if she felt uncomfortable here. "Mary, you know I do. There are too many bad memories. I really thought I'd never have to face this place again. Then the letter came, and you were determined to come here. I couldn't let you come alone. You are my niece, you're like my own child. I love you, and I will protect you."

Mary couldn't think of anything she needed to be protected from, but Pris was overly protective to begin with.

Pris noticed the time, "Mary, maybe we ought to turn in for the night."

But Mary persuaded Pris to play the piano for a while. Mary loved to hear Pris play. By the time they did retire to bed, Mary was very tired and ready for bed. Mary dropped off to sleep only to awake later to a cold room. It felt as if someone was there with her, but when she called out no one answered. She lit the candle at her bedside and looked around, but found no one. Nothing was out of place.

In the early dawn she fell into a deep sleep. When she finally awoke, the sun was already shinning. Mary dressed very slowly, she was so tired lately. Pris knocked on her door, "Mary, are you awake yet?"

"Yes, Pris. Come in."

"Mary, the supplies are coming over today. I think I shall go over to the mainland. Will you be alright here with Mrs. Bunt?"

"Don't worry so much."

After Pris left, Mary went down to the kitchen. "Good morning, Mrs. Bunt, sorry I'm so late. I feel so tired lately."

"Mary, you need to relax. Have some coffee and I'll fix you a good meal."

"Thanks, that sounds wonderful."

Mary decided that today she would ramble around the house, since she was still tired from missing so much sleep. When she finished breakfast, she went upstairs and started going from room to room.

There were eight rooms on the second floor. They were all used at one time as bedrooms or sitting rooms. There was dust everywhere from not being used over the years. Nothing but beds, dressers, and nightstands were in most of them. As Mary proceeded down the hall, she found a room that was locked. She would come back to it later. She knew there were some old keys hanging in the kitchen, maybe one would fit. When she started up to the next floor, she thought she saw someone going onto the upper landing. "Hello, is anyone there?"

No one answered. Mary went in search of the person she knew she had seen on another night, not to long ago. But when she searched she found no one. "I must really get some rest," she thought, "I'm seeing things that aren't even there."

CHAPTER FOUR

It was late afternoon and Mary realized she was very hungry. Mrs. Bunt fixed her a fruit salad, cold tea, and a ham sandwich. It was wonderful.

Mary was waiting for Pris at the dock to help with the supplies. It felt good to be outside. Mary told Pris of her adventures of the day and about the locked room. Pris assured her it was probably just another bedroom. Mary replied, “It shouldn’t be locked.”

“You’re adventurous, Mary. I remember being your age, I think you get that from me. My father said I was into everything.”

Mary only laughed, admittedly she was curious. Pris and Mary got the supplies to the house and put them away. Mary’s mind was still on the locked room upstairs. Mary told Pris again of the person she saw upstairs. “We need more lamps in the hallway, maybe it’s just shadows I’m chasing.”

Pris really wondered now what Mary was seeing, or not seeing. Beth once mentioned seeing things upstairs. Especially in her room, which Mary now occupied. But Mary refused to let anything scare her into moving out into another room. Pris and Mary lounged around the rest of the afternoon on the patio. Enjoying the smell of the sea and the flowers. Mary told Pris after dinner she was going up to her room to write some long overdue letters.

Pris agreed she needed to do the same thing. “Our friends must think we’ve disappeared from the face of the earth.”

“Pris, we’ve only been gone for two months, but I’m sure you’re right.”

Mary sat down at her desk to write letters and fell asleep. When Mary awoke, it was already dark in the room and cold again. Mary rubbed her eyes and looked around. There was a woman dressed in white standing by her bed. Mary gasped and the woman vanished. Mary was shaking very hard. She got up and ran out of the room to find Pris.

Pris was in the parlor when Mary ran in. She knew Mary was upset. Mary described the woman to Pris. She tried to make Mary believe that maybe she dreamed it. Mary wasn’t sure anymore what was real and what was imaginary.

Pris persuaded Mary to sleep in her room that night. Pris got up after Mary was sound asleep and went to Mary's room. She would sit there a while, just to see if anything happened. Soon Pris dozed off. Sometime later, she was aroused by a noise. Pris looked around the room. In the corner stood the woman. Pris called out and she vanished. Pris was very upset, she now knew the fear Mary felt. She needed to get Mary out of this room. Pris went to check on Mary, who was sound asleep. Pris stood guard over her niece the rest of that night.

At breakfast, Pris asked Mrs. Bunt if she had noticed anything strange since arriving on Singer Island. Mrs. Bunt said that she once heard walking on the third floor, but didn't dare go look.

"Well, at least I know Mary's not loosing her mind." Pris insisted, despite protests to the contrary, that Mary take the room next to her. Pris told Mary of the night's adventure. Mary was relieved when she heard Priscilla's account of her encounter of the mysterious woman. "We have to find out what or who is trying to scare us away Pris."

That morning, Mary went upstairs to the locked room, "There must be a key somewhere. I have to know what's in there." She examined the lock, but couldn't figure out how to jimmy it so it would open. She gave up for the moment and went in search of Pris, who was in the sitting room looking at a portrait of Charles. He was a very handsome man. He loved the island and it was so sad when he left. "Pris how long did Father live here?"

"Since he was a small boy, Mary. Our father bought this island before mother died. I've heard the servants talking about our mother being insane. They never knew I heard or understood any of their gossip."

"I really wish I'd known my father."

"He was a very loving and generous man."

"Pris, lets get the rakes and go to the family cemetery. I think we ought to clean the graves."

"Your grandfather is buried there too, along with your mother. The previous owners have plots there, a little ways from our family plot. Rumor has it that Barnamus was hanged on the other side of the island."

"Why was he hanged, Pris?"

"It's just an old story, not very interesting."

"Well, I'd like to hear it sometime."

Mary and Pris arrived in the graveyard about an hour later. Mary was looking around at the headstones when she came across the previous owner's grave. It read only "Barnamus Hillard. Hanged May 14,1738. Doomed to roam the earth with a restless soul." This puzzled Mary very much, but down deep in her heart it frightened her. "Pris, do you know anything about this headstone?"

"No, Mary. There were many stories, but I never really believed them. I often wondered what a man could have done that would deserve such a cruel remark on his headstone. Let's forget this and get to work. We have years of weeds and brush to remove."

Mary and Pris worked most of the afternoon each in solemn thought. Around four, Pris advised Mary maybe that they'd better quit for the day and go freshen up for dinner. "We can finish tomorrow, we accomplished quite a bit today."

"It does look much better."

When they arrived home, both women were dirty and tired. They were sore all over from hard physical labor. Neither was used to doing much of that at home. Their servants took care of the grounds. Even so, it felt good to be this tired. Mrs. Bunt told the ladies, there was time for a hot bath before dinner. Mary went upstairs to her room and prepared to undress.

Mrs. Bunt came in to draw her bath, "Mary, can I do anything else?"

"No, you're such a dear, I'm glad you're here with us. Do you know anything about the previous owner of the island, Barnamus Hillard?"

"I've only heard that he was hanged on the island and the curse they put on his headstone. It was a pity. The same people that accused him of being a warlock, put a curse on him."

Mary crawled into her bath and sat down thinking dreamily of the man she met on the boat to Savannah. "When did he slip my mind?" After soaking her sore muscles, she got out, dried off and dressed in a cool pink chiffon dress. She looked very good in pink and blue. They went well with her blonde hair and blue eyes.

She was a strikingly beautiful woman. She was very small framed. Pris often told her she looked like Beth. Mary went downstairs to dinner with Pris and Mrs. Bunt, now a part of the family.

Mrs. Bunt really outdid herself on this meal. It consisted of leg of lamb, fresh peas, mashed potatoes and gravy, and homemade buns, which Mary especially loved. They tasted like honey. With butter on top, they melted in your mouth. The meal was topped off with apple pie.

Mary hugged Mrs. Bunt and dropped a kiss on her cheek. “Pris and I are so lucky to have you here with us. We love you dearly.”

Mrs. Bunt was very touched and wiped a tear away. She never felt so needed or loved in her whole life. It felt good to belong somewhere finally. After dinner, Mary helped Mrs. Bunt clean up despite protests from Mrs. Bunt.

Pris went to the parlor to relax and read a good book. After they were finished, Mrs. Bunt retired and Mary went in search of Pris.

Pris lay her book aside and said to Mary, “We have a lot of catching up to do. We haven’t really talked in a long time.”

“I’ve missed our talks too.” They talked concerning there friends in Monet and wondered what they were doing.

Pris suggested, “We can go home anytime to see them.”

Mary didn’t want to leave just yet. “At least we can write them and catch up on all the news from home.” They both agreed to write letters home tonight.

Pris played the piano for Mary before they retired.

Mary sat down at her desk and tried to write letters, but she just couldn’t begin. Her mind was so full of the past, with everything from the previous four months. Her mind kept going around in circles. So, she finally decided to go to bed.

She fell asleep and dreamed of her mother. Her mother kept trying to warn her of something but she couldn’t hear what she was saying. She kept going further away. Mary was running trying to catch up with her mother, crying out, “Mother wait, please wait.”

Mary awoke crying like her heart would break in two. She cried into her pillow so she wouldn’t wake Pris. She got up, put on her robe, and went downstairs for a glass of warm milk.

Mrs. Bunt heard someone up and came to her door to see if she could help. She saw Mary was crying and came out to console her while her milk was warming. “Mary, dear sweet child, what’s got you so upset?” Mary told Mrs. Bunt about her dream. Mrs. Bunt’s heart went out to her.

“I really wish I had known her.” Mrs. Bunt sat up with Mary until she was nodding. Mrs. Bunt encouraged her to go back to bed and have sweet dreams. Mrs. Bunt went back to bed as well. Mary went upstairs, crossed over to her window and looked out across the lawn. She saw a shadow, then she saw the creature again. This time it stood still looking toward her room, her heart started beating fiercely. She was frozen in place, she couldn't move. Then the thing turned and ran back into the woods. Mary felt very cold. She knew it would be another sleepless night.

Mary slept late that morning since it was dawn before she fell asleep. She went downstairs around ten thirty.

Pris was in the kitchen. Mrs. Bunt filled Pris in on the previous night. "You're still not sleeping well at night?" inquired Pris solicitously.

"I've been having bad dreams Pris, so I got up for some warm milk. Mrs. Bunt kept me company." She decided not to tell Pris about what she saw, she didn't want to upset her. She felt as if the creature could read her thoughts and she sure didn't want to tell Pris about that feeling. "If I only knew what it was, or maybe who it was," she mused.

Today she decided to forget about it. She felt safe, it was daylight. Mary asked Pris, "What would you like to do today?"

"Well, let's see, we could go up in the attic and look through some old trunks."

"That sounds like fun, Pris. Let's go. There may be some of my mother's things up there." They were going through trunks when Mary came across a jewelry box. She opened it and found a locket. Mary held it up for Pris to see.

Pris recognized it immediately as belonging to Beth. But, she remembered Beth lost it before she died. How did it get up here? "Mary, that belonged to your mother, I remember it. But she lost it before she died."

"How did it get up here?"

"Mary, I have no idea. But I'm glad you've found it, your father gave it to her when she was pregnant with you." They looked through more trunks, they found portraits of ancestors, and clothes, that belonged to Mary's grandmother, Pris's mother. They went back downstairs for lunch and put her grandmother's diary in the parlor. They told Mrs. Bunt what they found. Mary was thrilled over her locket. She would cherish it for the rest of her life. They went back to the attic after lunch and rummaged through some more trunks. Mary found a lovely music box, it played the prettiest tune.

Mary asked Pris if she wanted it, or if she could keep it. Pris replied to her that she'd be glad for her to keep it. It was trimmed in gold with cherubs on top. It was truly lovely. They found some gowns that were worn to important balls. They carried a couple downstairs. They would have their housekeeper clean them.

On their way downstairs, they saw someone on the landing. They called out, but no one answered. They looked at each other and went in search of Mrs. Bunt.

They all searched the house but found no one inside. They decided to lock all the doors and windows. They agreed to keep them locked at all times. They stayed close together that day and remained indoors. Pris knew that something was definitely wrong. She felt it in her bones. She wanted, deep in her heart, to take Mary and run.

They agreed to keep their bedroom doors locked at night. All three women sat down to devise a plan of action. The only solution was to stay in at night and close to the house during the day. Little did they know that Mary couldn't do these things. Something was pulling at her at night, as if her will were not her own.

All reason was gone when she was being drawn to the island's cemetery. She couldn't help herself when she would rise to wander through the house and out the door, to wander the grounds, not really knowing she was going or why.

On one such night, she was near the lighthouse when she ventured off into the woods. There she came upon the ruins of a garden. She was sure that at one time it was beautiful, but now it was ghastly. She was not afraid. She felt at peace after a few moments in the garden. She sat down on a stone bench near a little pool, which was green with slime.

She sat, staring into the dark slimy water for a long time. Mary was out there for hours. She was being watched, how long or by whom she did not know. She would come back in the light of day, to see the little garden. She would make it beautiful again. She arose, returned to her room and fell into a deep sleep.

No one knew Mary was still wandering at night. Mary barely remembered herself. Mary stayed pretty close to the house during the day, but she often found herself standing in front of the locked room. She still hadn't found a key, or a way in.

CHAPTER FIVE

It was Monday, the day the boat was expected. Mary and Pris went to the dock to wait for the fisherman. They were going to Pineda to shop. Mary decided to go to the butcher and ask some questions about the island.

The butcher was more than happy to talk about the horrid events on the island. It wasn't often he got to tell the story. He might even add a thing or two of his own to make it more dramatic. He told Mary that people disappeared when they were on the island.

"People said Barnamus practiced witchcraft and used human sacrifices in his rituals. One of the townspeople's daughters came up missing. They got all riled up and went over to the island. They found him at a sacrifice altar, where he sacrificed animals, as well as people. They took him to the other side of the island and hanged him until he was dead.

"But he put a curse on the people before he died. He said anyone that owned the island, or lived there, would go insane and the insanity would be destructive to themselves and others. The people buried him and wrote on his marker that he was doomed to roam the earth with a restless soul.

"Every one was afraid of the island. For years it stood desolate, until your grandfather bought it and moved his family over there. He didn't believe in curses, or the unknown. Within a year after he bought the island, his wife gave birth to your father and soon become utterly insane.

"She killed herself or so it is told. They said she walked the floors at night, heard people calling her name when no one was around. Said her room stayed cold."

Mary felt a chill run up her back. She couldn't stand to hear anymore. She thanked him hurriedly and fled from the butcher shop in search of Pris. She was pale as a ghost when she found Pris. Pris asked what was wrong. She told Pris of the story from the butcher.

Pris was enraged, "Mary, I never wanted you to hear that from anyone. Your mother told me similar things while she was alive. That's when Charles took her away from the island for a few months. She settled down for a while so your father thought she was alright. While they were away, she became pregnant with you.

When they returned, Charles brought a doctor from the mainland to stay here to watch over her. She was incoherent most of the time, yelled out a lot to someone that wasn't there."

This upset Mary terribly, she never knew much about her mother. "Pris, why haven't you told me before what happened to mother?"

"I didn't want to hurt you dear, please, forgive me."

Mary was ready to return to the island, she was physically and emotionally spent. They returned to the house, Mary excused herself and went to her room to lie down for a while.

Pris was annoyed with the butcher and told Mrs. Bunt so. Mrs. Bunt agreed, "The butcher is a nosy gossip trying to frighten a young girl."

Mary laid down on her bed and wept for her mother's agony while here on the island. What really happened to her? Mary swore she'd find out. Mary slept for a time. When she arose, she freshened up for dinner.

Pris could tell she had been crying, her eyes were red and puffy. Pris ached for her niece. She wished she could help her, but she didn't know how. They ate their meal in silence, each with something different on her mind. Mary wondered how to find out what or who tormented her mother. Pris said to Mary that she never thought they'd ever come to this island and she never wanted to hurt Mary with these stories. "I wanted to protect you from this pain your feeling now."

"Pris, I really don't blame you. It's difficult hearing this from a stranger."

"I didn't want that to happen, Mary, I'm sorry."

"The butcher kept on about our family, even to the time I was born. I couldn't stand anymore. I ran out in search of you. Are there any other secrets I need to know before someone else tells me?"

"Mary, I'm not aware of any. I was so young myself. No one knew what was wrong with your mother, it saddened us deeply to see her going through so much pain. She was a very good woman and loved your father so much. Mary, think of her in this way no matter what people say about her. They knew nothing of her, only gossip.

"I will tell you what I know. After being here about a year, she began to roam the house and grounds at night. She told us something was keeping her awake. As if it were pulling at her mind and body. She couldn't control it. She said her room was consistently chilly. No one could explain this, except maybe it was from drafts. After Charles told Beth of the planned trip, we never heard anything else about her fears or the room. It was only after they returned that she got worse."

Mary needed to be alone for a bit, so she told Pris she was going for a short walk. She walked down the beach and thought of her room, the shadow in the hall, the creature she saw in the woods. Was she too losing her mind?

CHAPTER SIX

Mary finally fell into a fitful sleep, she dreamed of her mother. She was in a room that looked like Mary's. She was tied to the bed. She kept motioning for Mary to come to her. She pleaded with Mary to untie her. Mary stood looking at her not knowing what to do. She reached for the rope, but heard someone behind her screaming, "Don't untie that rope."

Mary sat straight up in her bed, trembling. She was wet with perspiration. She got up and went to the window. She felt so lonely and scared. She couldn't wait until morning. She felt better in the light of day.

Mary laid back down and drifted off to sleep again. She returned to the room in her dreams. Beth was still tied to the bed. Mary went to the bed and untied her. Beth came up off the bed reaching for her. Mary backed away with fright, her mother looked wild. She kept coming toward her. Just as she reached her Mary woke up in a panic.

She ran from the room screaming for Priscilla. Priscilla was frightened by Mary's screams. Mary ran into her aunt's room and threw herself into her arms, crying. It took hours for Priscilla to calm Mary, and find out what happened. Mary spent the rest of the night in Priscilla's bed.

When Mary awoke, she was tired, but dressed and went downstairs for breakfast. Priscilla was sitting at the table drinking coffee. She could see the strain on Mary's young face. Priscilla tried to get Mary to eat, but all she could manage was coffee and a roll.

Mrs. Bunt asked Mary how she slept, but she knew the answer before Mary spoke. It tore her heart out to see Mary so frightened and exhausted. Mary told Pris maybe she needed to get out for some fresh air. Priscilla told Mary she was going nowhere without her. They decided to go to the beach. Pris thought maybe that would relax Mary.

They strolled the beach for a while and then sat to rest. Mary looked out over the ocean and said to Pris, "Maybe we shouldn't have come to the island. But it's too late, now I can't leave until I have some answers." In a way Pris understood, she should have been stronger years ago and unraveled all these mysteries then. Perhaps this haunting would have stopped. Maybe now she could at least help Mary find the answers.

Mary suggested while they were out they should finish cleaning the graves. Pris didn't think that Mary should be in a place like that at that time, so she suggested a picnic at the lighthouse. Mary agreed to this. They went back to the house and fixed a nice lunch. They invited Mrs. Bunt along, but she declined the offer. She didn't want the house empty and she wanted to clean upstairs. Mary and Pris went off.

Mrs. Bunt started upstairs to dust and air out the rooms. She saw someone on the landing and screamed. She went back to the kitchen very shaken. Now she knew the fear Mary was carrying around. What was going on and why? She really hated being in the house alone, yet she was afraid to leave. She locked herself in the kitchen, away from the rest of the house and the worries of not knowing what was taking place.

Mary and Pris returned to the house to find Mrs. Bunt locked in the kitchen. Mrs. Bunt told them what she saw. "I didn't dare go looking alone, so I locked myself in."

"What are we going to do?"

"We must not be far from one another at anytime. There is safety in numbers." They moved Mrs. Bunt upstairs where she would be nearer to Pris and Mary. They didn't want her downstairs alone. They searched the house from top to bottom, all the windows were still locked, as were the doors. They found nothing out of the ordinary. No one was very hungry that night, they were just waiting for whatever or whomever to make another appearance.

Their nerves were on edge, they jumped at the least little noise. Mrs. Bunt and Priscilla knew they needed to pull themselves together for Mary's sake.

Mrs. Bunt asked Pris and Mary to call her Sara instead of 'Mrs. Bunt'. "I feel like a part of this family." This pleased the Windsors very much. She was very dear to both of them.

Sara offered to get some coffee for everyone, but Mary would not let her go alone. She decided that all three ought to go to the kitchen for coffee. Pris did not know what fear was. She felt this was all a little ridiculous, after all, she was a grown woman. Pris assured Mary she would be fine while the other two got coffee. Mary knew how stubborn Priscilla could be, so she went with Sara.

Pris looked around the room she spent so much time in as a child. It was cozy with a fireplace. She felt much better. When Mary and Sara returned, they enjoyed a cup of coffee. Each decided to read a book for a while. No one really cherished the thought of going upstairs. About eleven o'clock, everyone was exhausted so they went together upstairs to their rooms, the windows and doors were locked so they felt safe.

Mary got ready for bed and sat thinking of her secret garden. She made plans to clean the garden and restore the flowers. Mary still kept the garden a secret from Pris, for if she told her, she would also have to tell her how and when she found it. She thought about planting roses. She wanted to put them on her mothers grave.

She went to bed and fell asleep. She dreamed about her mother again. But she was on the grounds this time. She was walking through the garden. She was very beautiful.

Mary awoke early that morning and dressed. She didn't hear anyone stirring yet, so she crept down to the kitchen and started coffee. Somehow Mary would start on her garden today. She tried to figure how to get away from Pris and Sara, but could not come up with a plan.

Pris came through the door expecting to find Sara, but found Mary instead. "Your up early, did you sleep well?"

"I really don't remember. I suppose I did."

"I dreamed of my mother again last night. She was walking in a garden, she looked so happy."

Mary and Pris enjoyed a cup of coffee together. Sara joined them and apologized for not already having breakfast ready. Both were in agreement that was no problem. They were competent enough to do some things on their own. "We were up pretty late last night, and we were all very tired when we did get to sleep."

Sara fixed ham, bacon, eggs, and made Mary's favorite, hot buns. To everyone's amazement, they were all starved. Mary rambled around the house, she was getting edgy. "Pris I'm going for a walk on the beach. I can't stay inside like this any longer."

Pris understood, but it didn't make her feel any better about Mary going out on her own. Pris knew she couldn't keep Mary locked up inside forever. "Just be very careful Mary."

Mary went to the shed and got her garden tools. She walked down the path to the beach. It was good to be out of that house for a while, she felt safer for some reason. She walked the beach until she reached the path to the secret garden. There, she left the beach and walked into the wooded area, where the forgotten garden was. She started working diligently, weeding and digging in the soft earth. It smelled so good. Physical labor often helped her relax.

Mary accomplished a good deal of work and was feeling hungry. The time flew by, she didn't realize she'd been gone so long. She jumped up and ran back to the house. She was very dirty.

Pris met her at the door. Mary could see Pris was worried. "Mary, where have you been? You've been gone for hours! And look at your clothes and hands. What have you been doing?"

"I've been weeding Pris, I found this little garden off the beach down the way. I want to fix it up again."

"I remember that garden Mary. It used to be a beautiful place. It belonged to your mother. I guess the years have really taken their toll on it."

"It could be a lovely place. I finished the weeding, now I have to remove the brush and plant some flowers. I will make it beautiful again."

"That's good Mary, it will give you something to do."

CHAPTER SEVEN

Mary received a letter from Henry telling of a visit by the end of the month. She could have the garden ready and take him to see what she had accomplished. She would also take him to see the lighthouse and the graveyard. She would get him to go to the other side of the Island with her to investigate the buildings she noticed when she was at the lighthouse.

Pris brought her back to the present by showing her a seashell. "When storms brew up, Mary, you can find all kind of shells. It will be time for the spring storms soon. Then you will find all sorts of fascinating things along the beach."

Mary thought about the weather in a different way. She knew she would be forced to stay in more, due to the storms. Then she could find a way into the locked room. Mary went upstairs and cleaned up.

When she came down, she and Pris took a stroll to the graveyard. When they returned, Sara wasn't there, that was very odd and they were worried. Maybe she went out for some fresh air. She hardly left the house. About an hour later, they saw Sara coming out of the woods in a very big hurry. Sara came through the door as Pris and Mary entered the kitchen. Pris asked Sara if everything was alright. She replied, she was fine. But Mary thought she looked different. They didn't question her because her own personal life was none of their business.

"Dinner will be ready soon. I'm sorry it's late."

"Sara, don't worry about that. Take your time, we're in no hurry," responded Mary.

Mary and Pris went upstairs to freshen up. Mary went across to her window and sat down and thought, "What's happening to me? All my life things have been pleasant and I was in control. I never dreamed things would be like this." Mary decided to go back to the attic and look some more. "Maybe there's a clue to the strange goings on in the house."

Pris knocked on her door. Mary told her to come in. "What are you thinking about?"

"All the things that have happened since we arrived, the locked room with no key, the shadow of a person in the hall at night."

"Mary, you've got to put all this out of your mind and get some rest."

"Priscilla, I was going to the attic to look around again. Maybe we will find some answers there. Would you like to come with me?"

"Mary, I hate to think of you going anywhere alone, even in this house. We'll go up and look after dinner. Maybe we need to stay in this evening and rest. We have been doing a lot of exploring and the work in the graveyard has been very tiring."

Mary and Pris went to the attic that evening for the second time, still with no idea what they were looking for. They found nothing that would explain anything.

Mary was exhausted and told Pris she was going to bed early. As she was drifting off to sleep, she thought of Barnamus. Then she fell into a deep sleep where she was riding on a cloud. She could see the whole island below and a crowd of people running around. They were hanging someone. On closer inspection, she saw it was a young man with long hair and a beard. She knew instantly that it was Barnamus Hillard. She was reliving the scene of a lynch mob.

Mary awoke with a start and found herself in bed. It was almost morning and she lay awake thinking. She would not give up until she found a clue. She dressed and went down to breakfast. Mary couldn't wait until Pris woke up. She wanted to start looking as soon as possible.

Pris came down around eight thirty and was surprised that Mary was already up. "Pris I want to go to the attic again this morning. I hope I find something up there." She told Pris about the dream. Pris wasn't surprised. They looked all morning, there were so many trunks to go through. Mary noticed an old wardrobe. She kept looking and came across a journal of events in the early 1700's.

Pris was looking in an old trunk and found Grandma Windsor's diary. "Mary, I've found something." They were thrilled with what they found. "Maybe we'll find some answers. We'll read some tonight after dinner. Let's go down to the study for a while."

While they were in the attic, a storm was coming in. By the time they reached the ground floor, it was getting dark from the storm. The wind was howling. It began to thunder and lightening in the distance. "Looks like we're in for a good one. Mary, let's check the windows to make sure they're closed tight." The storm grew worse by dinner. The wind was howling so fiercely it made everyone jumpy. Mary wasn't looking forward to going to bed tonight. After dinner Pris, Mary, and Sara went into the parlor to sit in front of the fire to drink their coffee. "Well Mary, let's get down to some reading."

Sara asked what they had found. Mary told her about the letters, journals and the diary.

Mary sat reading a letter, "Pris, did you know our family knew the Hillards? There's a letter here to your father from the Hillard family. The letter is dated 1743, it doesn't say much. It's from a relative of Barnamus Hillard. It says they were very interested in his offer to buy the island and they were looking forward to meeting with him."

"Grandfather bought the island in 1743 from the Hillards?"

"That means we've owned the island for fifty-eight years. What's in the diary Pris?"

"It is dated January 1743. Edward Windsor is thinking about buying an island. He has received word from Jeffery Hillard that they were pleased with his offer. Edward has wanted the island for a long time, I don't know why it is so important to him.

"March 1743: Edward has bought Singer Island and we have come to live on the island with our servants.

"April 1743: The island is simply breath taking, we have the servants set up now in their quarters. We furnished the house with beautiful pieces. The furniture that was here was ghastly. I'm looking forward to having more children to enjoy the island with Priscilla and Charles. They are enjoying roaming the beaches and the woods around the house. We rarely see them except for their lessons and meals. Edward has started building additional servant quarters. The living space was terrible for those poor people. There is a lighthouse on the far end of the island to which I enjoy going.

"May 1743: We have been here three months and it is heaven. Edward has bought a few horses and brought them over to our island, I ride daily around the shores of the beach. I have found a perfect spot for a garden, I will plant a variety of flowers, when I'm finished it will be beautiful. I will keep it secret and it will be my own personal hideaway.

"June 1743: I have begun work on the garden, it is beginning to take shape. I have roses, tulips, and marigolds among various other plants. I enjoy coming to my garden, it gives me a sense of peace.

"Mary it's getting late, we should be going to bed."

"It is late, but at least we're learning about the island from your mother. Do you remember much of your childhood here Pris?"

"Yes, quite a bit anyway, up to where Charles was born and moving here. I remember it didn't seem long after we moved here that mother died. It's tragic, we both lost our mothers here on the island."

The ladies proceeded to get ready for bed making sure all doors and the windows were locked before going up for the night. Mary got ready for bed, she blew out the candle and crawled into bed, exhausted. Tomorrow she would read more of her grandmother's diary.

Three hours after Mary went to bed, she awoke. Her candle was burning and her door was open. She knew she had closed and locked the door and extinguished the candle before going to bed. She was scared and curious at the same time. Someone must have been in her room when she went to bed. She jumped out of bed and ran to Priscilla's room banging on her door and yelling, "Pris, wake up."

Pris was startled awake by her niece's screams, "I'm coming Mary." Pris opened the door and Mary ran inside.

"Pris, I woke up and my candle was burning and my door was standing open. Pris, I locked that door, I know I did. And I blew out the candle before crawling into bed. Someone must have been in my room when I entered and got ready for bed. Or came in after I was asleep. But how did they get in, and who was it?"

"Let's check the house and check on Sara to be sure she is alright."

They knocked on Sara's door and she got up immediately and put on a robe and opened the door. She was informed of Mary's incident. "We're going to search the house."

Sara agreed it should be checked. They searched and found no one. Sara made coffee for them, commenting, "Pris, if someone was here they didn't leave by the doors or windows." They were really frightened, but didn't know what to do about it. They stayed up drinking coffee for the rest of the night.

By daylight they were very tired, so they decided to try to take a short nap. They could not go day and night too, that would get the better of all of them. They agreed to watch over the one who slept while the other two were up together. Mary could not go back upstairs yet, so she used the sitting room to take a nap. Mary slept for two hours. When she awoke there was a tray with coffee and buns. She was so hungry, so she sat up and ate two buns and drank her coffee.

Pris came in and asked if she rested any at all. Pris planned to take a nap after lunch and let Sara take one now.

Mary decided to read some more of the diary later in the evening. "August 1743: Two nights ago, I heard someone walking the hall. I arose and found no one. I told the servants to make sure all the doors and windows were locked.

"September 1743: One night I awoke to find the candle on my nightstand burning. I knew I blew it out upon retiring. Strange things have begun to occur with no discernible reason. I have moved my children in the room next to mine, with their nanny for safety. Edward believes it's my imagination, but I know it's not.

"October 1743: I'm having trouble sleeping, I'm roaming the floors at night. I can't sleep, expecting at any time for something to happen, but I have no idea what. I hear people walking, and even a scream now and then. Things are worse, I saw a woman on the third floor landing. Nanny swears she hears nothing.

"November 1743: Well, things have quieted down, I'm sleeping a little better, and I haven't heard anything in the house for three weeks. Things are better between Edward and myself. I'm getting some of my color back and putting on a little weight. I spend a lot of time in my garden in the sunshine. I'm still riding daily. The children are flourishing wonderfully.

"January 1744: I have been visited twice by a lady in a white dress in my room. I'm falling apart little by little. She never utters a word, just looks at me with the most pitiful, saddest eyes I've ever seen. I haven't told Edward of these visits, he's been through enough with me. I really don't know how much more I can endure."

"Pris, that is the end of your mother's diary. She experienced everything I have."

"It looks like it did get too much for her, she took her own life. They said she threw herself off the bluff on the east end of the island. I don't believe the stories, I believe she slipped or someone pushed her to her death. From what I remember, she just didn't seem to be the kind of person to kill herself. She was full of love and laughter and joy. My father was a hard man, and he believed the stories. He never forgave her and ignored me and Charles after her death. I guess me more than Charles, because I looked like her in every detail. The servants and Charles were my family until Beth came into our lives."

"Priscilla, there is something definitely strange about this place, and I swear I'm going to get to the bottom of it."

"Mary, young ladies do not swear."

"I'm sorry Pris. But it has taken too many of my family away and I won't stand for it."

"Mary, let's forget this for a while. Let's calm down and take a walk to clear our heads."

They were walking on the beach and Pris stopped and looked at Mary. Mary stopped and looked back, "What's wrong Pris?"

"After everything you've seen and heard you still won't leave?"

"No! I'm more determined to put too many wrongs right for a change. Running never solves anything. You taught me that Pris. This family has run long enough."

"Mary, I'm fifty-eight year's old and maybe your right. I should have come back years ago."

Pris was born May 3,1738, Charles was born June 17, 1740. Pris was the oldest and she thought Charles was her charge. Everywhere she went, she took Charles. She loved him dearly. Charles was 56 years old when he died here on the island. Charles came back here for some reason unknown to Pris or Mary. Charles was buried here on the island in 1796. Only the preacher and Mrs. Bunt were present, but Pris or Mary knew nothing of her presence.

CHAPTER EIGHT

Mary's weight continued to drop under the stress she was experiencing. Many nights Pris awoke to hear Mary rambling around in her room, at least she thought it was Mary. Mary still hadn't given up the idea of getting into that one locked room. Sara was also worried. She talked to Pris about taking Mary away, but she knew in her heart it was useless. Mary would never agree to go.

Mary would not leave until she found some answers. Mary became withdrawn, which confused and scared Pris. They were inseparable. Mary stayed pretty much to herself now. Pris decided not to push. She didn't want to drive her further away. Mary spent a lot of her time in her garden.

She had seen the creature three more times since the night at her bedroom window. It didn't seem as frightened of her as before, but she still couldn't make out what it was.

Mary roamed the island more and more, enjoying its beauty and serenity. On one such outing she came across Barnamus's altar. She froze and looked around, then hurried away. The place felt familiar and she didn't like that feeling. Visions flashed through her mind.

She saw a very handsome man leaning over her telling her of his love. It was a love one only felt or dreamed of once in a lifetime. She had never been in love before, so how she wondered did she know how it felt. Suddenly she felt a longing in her heart for someone she didn't even know. And the worst feeling was, she didn't think she'd ever feel this kind of love again.

She found herself at the altar often, not knowing what was pulling her there, but needing to be near this place. She didn't understand in her heart. She couldn't tell Pris of this feeling she felt here at the altar. She would keep it to herself.

The feeling was very strong of having lived before, a long time ago. She knew this place so well. When she was asleep, she dreamed disturbing dreams of the altar and the man she loved. Nothing about her dreams was very clear to her.

Mary decided to invite Pris to her garden. She often cut fresh flowers to take to the family graves. She planned a picnic for her aunt the next day. The appointed day was clear, warm, and lazy. Pris was pleased with Mary's suggestion . They couldn't have asked for a nicer day.

It seemed like months to Pris since they shared time together. Pris was very surprised at the work Mary put into the garden. She told her how proud she was of her accomplishment.

"I come here for hours, Pris. It's so peaceful."

"I've wondered where you've been spending so much time."

"Sometimes when I can't sleep I come here. I feel safer, I can't explain it but that's how I feel."

Pris dropped the subject. She wanted nothing to spoil this day with her niece. They ate their lunch. They spread a blanket on the ground and just lounged around for the afternoon. Mary informed Pris that she wanted to know every inch of the island. "It's especially beautiful at daybreak and sunset. Pris, lets get up early tomorrow and go exploring. We can see most of the island tomorrow and return again later."

"I would enjoy that. I get lonely at the house without you. I know Sara's there, but she's not you. You've kept pretty much to yourself lately. I didn't want to pry, or push you. I figured you needed some time to your self."

"I'm sorry, I didn't realize I was that bad. Please forgive me. I'd never cut you out of my life." They started home around three o'clock, walking slowly up the beach.

"Mary, there's a storm brewing again. It looks like it's going to be a good one. We need to get home and close everything up."

"In that case, we can ramble around the house some more, and I can look for the key again. I sure would like to find that key for my own curiosity. Aren't you curious Pris? What did Father lock away in there?"

"Mary, you're letting your imagination get the best of you. But we will look for the key, it might be fun."

When they arrived home Mary went upstairs to change. She quickly became accustomed to the drafts in the house. When storms blew through the winds became chilly. She entered her room and stopped dead still. Someone had strewn all her belongings all over the room.

She flew downstairs in search of Sara and Priscilla. They went upstairs together and looked around. They went to Mary's room, the only thing missing was Mary's locket that had been left on her dresser. “Pris someone took my mothers locket, I wouldn’t wear it outside the house. I was afraid I’d loose it, and now it’s gone.”

Mary sat down and cried. Pris and Sara consoled her. “That’s all I owned of hers.” Sara sent them downstairs while she straightened Mary’s room. Sara came down and Mary asked if she heard anything while they were out.

She told Mary and Pris that she went for a walk right after they left. “It was so nice outside, I needed a breath of fresh air.”

“I hate knowing someone handled my things and took my locket.”

Sara went to fix dinner, leaving Mary and Pris to ponder the break in. This was one more mystery to solve. After dinner, everyone went to the parlor. Sara apologized for leaving the house. They both assured her it was alright. Sara needed to get out too.

“We can’t expect you to stay in all the time. Mary, I think you should have a glass of wine, it will calm your nerves.”

“I think we all need one. I need something to calm me down. Pris can I sleep in with you tonight?”

“Of course you can, Mary. I don’t want you to be alone.” The strain of the past two months was taking its toll on Mary’s physical and mental health.

Two long months of not sleeping much and having hardly any appetite was beginning to show in her clothes. They were becoming loose on her. Priscilla decided to ask Doctor Jennings to prescribe something to help Mary sleep.

At last, too exhausted to stay awake, they went to bed. Mary fell asleep and dreamed of her lover from the past. She tossed and turned all night. Pris knew something was bothering her even while she slept.

Mary arose, dressed slowly and went to the kitchen. Sara was already up with coffee brewing, Mary needed some bad. Pris came down later looking tired. Mary felt bad about keeping Pris awake during the night. She would sleep in her room tonight regardless of what was happening. She couldn’t put Pris through any more restless nights.

Pris asked Mary if she wanted her to take in her dresses. “You’ve lost so much weight.”

Mary told Pris she would help. Neither one felt like going out today. They would stay in and sew. Pris told Mary of the days when she and Charles had roamed the island.

"They were the best times of our lives. We were free spirited. We'd play pirates, tell ghost stories, Charles would even play dress up with me at times. Back then we never dreamed our island would cause so much pain."

"Don't think about it Pris, let's just relax." They finished the dresses and went to the kitchen to help Sara. They enjoyed her company.

Mary walked out of the kitchen while Pris and Sara were talking. She wanted to find her locket. She would look all over the house. She checked the parlor, the bedrooms and, by chance, she went to the attic.

She was roaming around when she saw something lying on the wardrobe. She went over and there lay her locket. She ran downstairs to the kitchen where Pris and Sara were. "Please come to the attic with me, hurry."

Pris and Sara were not aware Mary had been up in the attic alone. They went up together and Mary showed them her locket lying on the wardrobe. Everyone turned pale and found a place to sit down. "How did it get here? It was on my dresser the day my room was disturbed." No one could answer that question. It was getting late, Mary picked up her locket and put it around her neck, where it would stay.

Everyone went back to the kitchen where they sat and talked about the nights events. Pris asked Sara, "Is there anyone on the mainland who could be playing pranks on us?" But Sara couldn't think of anybody who would do that.

Everyone Sara knew was afraid of the island. She wondered if it were him, just wanting to be close to Mary, not meaning to scare her. She couldn't mention her secret to Pris or Mary, no matter how much she loved them. She made a promise a long time ago, and she couldn't break that confidence.

Mary went to the parlor to read a while till lunch was ready. Mary delayed going to bed that night, but finally couldn't stay awake any longer. She went to bed and fell asleep. It felt so good to sleep a whole night through.

The next morning she dressed feeling revived. This morning there was color in her cheeks again. She was anxious to go exploring. Pris didn't feel up to going, but finally let Mary go, with the promise she wouldn't go far.

She went through the woods, crossed a couple of streams, and came out in a clearing. There stood the building she spotted from the light house. She rambled around inside. It was dusty, but it was still furnished. It could be made nice with a little work. That gave her an idea.

She wanted some horses and this would be the perfect place for the stable hand to stay. She would discuss this with Pris. There were horses here before, she remembered Pris talking about them. She went in search of the stables. They were not too bad, bridles and saddles were hanging inside. They needed a little repairing but nothing a man couldn't fix.

When Mary got back to the house, she told Pris of her idea about getting a couple of horses for them to ride. Priscilla told Mary they could have a couple brought over, she enjoyed riding her self. "That's a splendid idea, we will hire a man to help around the grounds and I will feel better having a man on the island with us. We will go to the mainland the next time the boat brings our supplies and buy two of their best horses."

Mary was very excited about the thought of having a horse to ride over the island. She could cover more of the island that way. Mary told Pris she was going down on the beach in search of shells. She had found quite a few beautiful shells, since arriving on the island. The storms washed them up on shore. After searching for a while she returned to the house, glad to show off her finds. As she was hurrying home, the wind began to blow and it began to rain. Mary made it just before a torrent of rain started.

Mary showed Sara and Pris her shells, then went upstairs to freshen up. She sat down on the bed and, before she knew it she was sound asleep. Pris woke her two hours later. Mary apologized for falling asleep.

Pris told her it was good that she was able to take a nap. "I shouldn't have awakened you, but you haven't eaten since breakfast. You need some nourishment."

"I have to admit, it's the best sleep I've had in a while." She arose and freshened up for dinner. Sara, Mary and Pris sat around the cozy kitchen table eating. Sara was included in every meal, she was more than a servant, she was family. After dinner they sat in front of the fireplace planning their trip into Pineda for the horses.

Sara told them of a kind man who might come to the island to live and work. He was in his mid-fifties. His name was Mathew Long. He was born in Pineda and married to a local girl for twenty-five years. His wife had come down with scarlet fever and died about four years earlier.

"He raised two sons and two daughters, but they grew up and moved away. Now they have families of their own." He was a very lonely man, and he was very good at building. "He could restore the stables, and it would be nice to have a man around."

"We would all feel safer, I know I would. Tomorrow we will find him while we're shopping and see if he would be interested in working for us here. But for now the hour is late and we need our rest."

They went to bed around ten. Mary's dreams usually started around midnight so she got a couple of hours sleep before her terror began. A few hours after she went to bed, she heard someone walking in the hall. She got up and went to the door and stood very still listening. She heard someone going down the hall. Mary opened the door very slowly and entered the hall, looking both ways. She didn't see anyone, so she started down the hall to the stairs that went up to the next floor. She stopped and looked up the stairs, someone was standing on the landing. That's all she remembered, she fainted.

CHAPTER NINE

Mary came too a little while later remembered seeing someone on the landing, got up and ran to her room, locking the door behind her. She didn't know how long she lay at the foot of the landing before she came too. It was a woman, she was sure of that, there was a strange light illuminating her. But Mary didn't know who it was.

She felt chilled to the bone, and her cold room didn't help matters any. She crawled into bed and pulled the covers up to her chin, there would be no more sleep for her tonight. She would not tell Pris or Sara about her visitor.

When morning arrived she dressed, and went up to the third floor to look around. Everything was in place. Why was this person standing at the landing? She went down to the kitchen for breakfast. Today would be the day they would go to Pineda in search of two riding horses, and to meet Mr. Long. The day would be a full one.

There was no trouble finding the horses and making arrangements for them to be brought to the island. Mary went in search of Mr. Long, to see if he'd work for her. She liked him instantly, as he did her. They agreed on a salary, and that he would come over with the horses. Mary was feeling more like her old self, she stopped and bought gifts for Pris and Sara. Pris received a pretty bonnet and Sara got a shawl for her shoulders. She picked up a few personal things for herself then went in search of her aunt to return home.

Sara was glad to see them, she really didn't like being alone since Mary started seeing someone in the house. She kept busy, so her imagination wouldn't run wild with her.

They ate lunch and Mary took a long overdue nap. She dreamed of Henry, he was so handsome. She wished he'd visit soon, so she could have someone to roam the island with that was more her own age.

She awoke and stretched lazily, when she arose she drew herself a hot bath, and soaked for a while. She washed her hair, and was sitting in the window letting the sun dry her golden curls. The sun was so warm, she dreaded the thought of winter coming, because she would be inside more. She wouldn't think about that now. It was still a couple of months until winter came. She'd enjoy what was left of her summer. Now that Mr. Long was coming to stay she felt much better.

He could cut enough wood to get them through the winter. It didn't get extremely cold, there was just the dampness from the ocean.

It was almost dinner so Mary dressed and went downstairs. Sara was putting the finishing touches to the table when Pris came in from the kitchen. They prepared a delicious meal and Mary was famished.

Both ladies noticed the glow on Mary's face and were overjoyed to see her smile. Mary was excited about the horses and Mr. Long coming to join them here on the island. Sara was a friend of this man and knew he would take care of these two fine ladies.

After coffee they went to the parlor to sit for a while until time for bed. Mary was still very tired so she excused herself and went upstairs. She slept until around one a.m., when she heard a squeak on the stairs, and went to investigate. On her way she stopped and woke Pris. "Pris I heard a squeak on the stairs, please come with me to see what it is."

"Let's be very quite and walk slowly to the stairs." Mary asked Pris "Do you hear the noise?"

"Yes, Mary, I do. Lets look and see if we see anyone." They caught a glimpse of a woman in a long flowing dress running up the stairs. They were not prepared to follow her, due to the hour and the poor lighting, so they went back to Priscilla's room and locked the door and settled in for the rest of the night. It would be another long one.

Sara's door was closed so they expected her to still be sleeping when they came down, but she wasn't in the house. Mary and Pris fixed bacon, eggs, coffee and biscuits for breakfast. They were sitting at the table when Sara walked in from outside. They looked at each other with a puzzled expression on their face. Sara immediately apologized for not having the meal ready.

"We thought you were still asleep Sara. Mary and I would have been worried sick about you if we had known you were outside. Last night our ghostly visitor was back." They filled Sara in on their sleepless night while they finished their breakfast.

Mary decided to stay inside today, she was going to check out the third floor and see if they missed something in their search. She knew that they were seeing someone, but were they dead or alive? Mary checked closets, walls, under beds, and still turned up nothing. Mary thought there might have been a trap door that no one knew about.

The day passed quickly, and before she realized it, dinner was being placed on the table.

Pris, Mary, and Sara sat in the study for a while enjoying the fire. Mary loved sitting before a fire, it gave a feeling of peace and tranquility. Mary told Pris she was going on up to get ready for bed, Pris told her she would check on her before turning in.

Mary was standing by her window when someone opened her door. She turned around and nobody was there. She called out to Pris and Sara but received no answer.

Mary ran down stairs like the devil himself were after her. "Pris, Sara where are you?"

"I'm here in the study Mary, what's wrong?"

"Have you been upstairs?"

"No, Mary. Why?"

"Someone opened my door while I was looking out my window."

"Let's go ask Sara, maybe she didn't want to disturb you."

Mary and Pris found Sara quickly and asked about the door. "No, I haven't been upstairs since breakfast. Are you sure you didn't leave it open dear?"

"No, I'm sure I closed it."

"Well, you don't really remember Mary, so let's not get upset alright."

"Maybe your right Pris, I don't remember things lately."

Mary went back to the study and sat down in front of the fire for a while. What in the world was happening to her? Pris was sure Mary knew what she was talking about, she just didn't want to upset her any more than she already was. She decided to stand guard over her from this point on. If Mary was going crazy, they'd go there together.

When Mary went to bed Pris set up a cot outside her bedroom door. If Mary got up, she'd have to go through her before she left the room. The night went well, Pris was not awakened by Mary that night. When Mary arrived in the kitchen Pris asked her how she slept.

"I slept better than I have in months."

"You even look better this morning Mary. How about a walk in the garden after breakfast?"

"Sure, sounds great." They went to the cemetery after they left the garden. The storm left quite a bit of debris. They picked up limbs, and decided they needed rakes and a shovel to finish the job.

By this time they had worked up an appetite, so they headed toward the house. Both agreed on something like sandwiches, some fruit and a cool drink. First they needed to wash some of the dirt off . Mary really enjoyed the day out with Pris. At Priscilla's age she could pretty well keep up with Mary at anything they did. This contributed to their close bond, Priscilla didn't feel like an aunt to Mary, but a best friend. Mary was glad her father picked Pris to raise her, but she still would have wanted to know her father.

She finished and went downstairs. This was only one day of many that Pris would accompany Mary on her outings.

After lunch they went into the study where Mary found an interesting book and curled up on the sofa with it and fell sound asleep. Pris checked their finances while Mary was asleep. Sara was in the kitchen making apple pies for dinner. Pris joined her while Mary slept. Pris was feeling the strain of all the events that were happening lately. She began to feel very tired and she didn't know why, because she slept very heavily lately. Mary awoke and strolled into the kitchen, she was very happy about the horses, since purchasing them Mary mentioned nothing about her room, or the woman in white. Pris told Mary they would go to the stable and try to clean it up as much as possible before the horses arrived.

The next morning they were up bright and early headed for the stable. There was a lot of work to be done, Pris only hoped she and Mary could handle it. At least it was keeping them busy, and Mary seemed more like her old self. By lunch they accomplished quite a bit. There was some carpentry work still to be done, but she figured Mr. Long could handle that. They were expecting Mr. Long over from Pineda tomorrow. They worked all evening and stopped just before dinner to go wash up. Mary wasn't really in the mood to eat, but she knew she needed to, so she could keep up her strength. After the meal was over, everyone went into the parlor. Priscilla played the piano for a while enjoying the rhythm of the piece she was playing.

Mary began to doze off so Pris encouraged her to go to bed. The next morning Mary was pleasantly surprised, waiting for her was the young man she met on the ship. Henry came over with Mr. Long to see Mary and her aunt.

"Mr. Collins it is a pleasure to see you again."

"Well, Miss Windsor I promised you ladies a visit on my return trip."

"You must stay with us, we have plenty of room."

"Thank you, that would be nice." Pris was talking to Mr. Long while Mary filled Henry in on the last five months.

"Mary do you think its wise for three females to be here alone?"

"Well, no, but no one will come to the island."

"Maybe while I'm here I can find you some help."

"I hope you have better luck, Sir, than we have had."

Mary asked Henry if he would like to look around. "I would love to, it's such a huge island."

"Yes, I know I've been here five months and I still haven't seen all of it."

"I'd love to see it with you Mary, I've thought about you often since we first met. I'd like to get to know you better."

"Thank you, Henry, I'd like to get to know you better, too. Consider yourself a guest of Singer Island."

Pris joined Henry and Mary on the patio. "Well Mary, we have a stableman, he will stay in one of the rooms off the house until the servants quarters are ready."

"Pris, Henry will be staying as a guest for a while."

"How wonderful! Now we will have two men here with us for protection."

"What are you talking about Miss Windsor?"

"We will fill you in on the past five months later, Henry, after dinner." Sara cooked a wonderful meal, she outdid herself on the apple pie. Both men raved about her cooking. When dinner was finished they went to the study. Pris proceeded to tell them of the appearance of a woman in the house up on the third floor. The men looked at each other with concern in their eyes. After Pris finished filling them in, it was quite late, so Pris suggested everyone turn in for the night. That night no one heard or saw anything out of the ordinary.

They arose early ate breakfast and set off for the house near the stables. Both men agreed that they needed to start work immediately so that it would be ready when the horses arrived. They poked around looking at lumber until around noon, and stopped to go to the main house and eat lunch.

Mary knew it wouldn't take much for her to fall in love with Henry. He was so handsome, he stood around six foot tall with sandy blonde hair and hazel eyes. His appearance was rugged, which became him.

When they got to the house they all went to freshen up. Pris could see the attraction between her niece and Henry already. For the first time in months, Pris felt some relief from the nightmare of the island.

They all enjoyed their lunch and went to the parlor for a while before returning to work. Henry was thinking about the story Pris told about the woman and he decided to keep an eye on Mary. Henry and Mathew went back to the stable to replace some boards to keep the horses in their stalls. It was easy to work with Mathew, he was a very skilled carpenter, and very friendly. "I could tell he was lonely and enjoyed my company. I enjoyed his also," thought Henry. They accomplished quite a bit that day, it was getting late and they knew they needed to go wash up before the evening meal.

On the way back to the house they encountered the creature. Henry asked Mathew, "What, in heavens name, was that?"

Mathew said "It beats me, I've never seen such in my life. There are some strange stories about this island, but I never believed any of them."

"Well, we'll find out what's going on here, the ladies safety depends on us."

Neither Henry nor Mathew ever mentioned to Pris or Mary their encounter with the creature on their way to the house. They all went to bed early that night because a lot of work needed to be done in a very short time. Henry's room was across the hall from Mary's. If anything went on he was sure he'd hear it. Mary went to bed and fell into a disturbed dream.

Again she dreamed of the lynch mob, this time there was a young girl crying softly off to the side where she couldn't be seen. Mary thought she knew the girl, her heart went out to her. Mary awoke in a cold sweat, the girl's presence disturbed her. Mary knew her from somewhere. She arose and walked around the room, hoping not to awaken anyone.

But a knock sounded on her door, and Henry was standing there. "Is everything alright Mary, I heard you stirring around in here and wanted to make sure you were not in peril." Henry noticed Mary was very pale. "Mary lets go down and have a glass of warm milk, maybe that will help you get back to sleep. If you feel like talking I'm a good listener."

Mary got her robe and they went to the kitchen. Henry noticed that Mary was quiet and somewhat withdrawn. But he didn't want to force her to talk before she was ready. He wanted her trust above everything else. They sat and made small talk for a while, then Mary opened up to him. Mary told Henry about the dream that night and of previous ones since coming to the island. “Henry I don’t feel in control of myself at times, and it frightens me.”

Henry knew he would stay close to her from then on. Henry realized he wanted to protect her from whatever sinister thing was plaguing her, these haunting experiences were getting too much for her. Henry persuaded Mary to take Laudanum to help her rest and go back to bed. Henry was up the rest of the night wondering how to help Mary. He knew now he was falling in love with her.

Next morning he talked to Pris about the previous night. Pris felt at ease now that someone was here to help with Mary. “Henry she hasn’t slept much since coming here. You can tell the weight she’s lost and the circles under her eyes. And she refuses to leave.”

“We’ll just keep a close watch on her.”

After breakfast Henry and Mathew headed for the stables. Mary was still sleeping, so they didn’t wake her for the outing.

Pris was in the parlor when Mary came downstairs. She couldn’t remember why she felt so groggy . She poured a cup of coffee and sat down on the couch. “Where’s Henry, Pris?”

“He’s already working at the stables. He thought you needed to rest after last night.”

“What happened last night, I remember going to bed early. Everything’s so hazy.”

“Henry said you woke him last night pacing your room. He knocked on your door to see if you were alright. You had another bad dream Mary about Barnamus Hillard. Henry gave you some warm milk and a sleeping potion.”

“That explains why I’m so groggy, Pris, because of the medicine. After I finish my coffee why don’t we take a stroll on the beach. It’s to nice too stay inside.”

Pris needed to get out too, she thought maybe they could go to the garden. Mary had restored the garden to its original majestic beauty. They went upstairs and changed into more appropriate clothing for the garden work. The garden was just drying out from the previous nights dew. Water dripped from the leaves of the trees and from the flowers. They set in weeding the garden and trimming the hedges around the wall. Mary cut fresh flowers for the house. She thought it might cheer the place up some.

CHAPTER TEN

As soon as Mary and Pris returned home, Henry and Mathew came in for lunch. Henry commented on Mary's flowers. "It must have taken quite an effort to raise such beautiful roses."

Mary told him about restoring the garden.

"It looks like you've been very busy since you came here."

"Yes, I've cleared the family cemetery also, but there's lots more to be done to make everything as it once was."

"With your determination, Mary, you'll get it done before you realize it's all done." Everyone ate a light lunch and sat resting on the patio for the best part of the evening. Henry asked Mary if she would like to take a walk. Mary told him she'd be happy too. They walked down the lane toward the dock. Mary felt uneasy at the spot where she'd seen the creature before. She told Henry of that experience, and what it looked like. He decided to search the island for the creature soon. His curiosity got the best of him.

Henry knew that there was an explanation for what Mary saw, and he would find it. Mary also told Henry of the appearances in the upstairs hall on several occasions. They reached the docks and stood watching the sun set. Henry told Mary they needed to get back before it got darker, for they carried no lamps with them. The moon wouldn't shine that night because of the haze over the ocean.

They returned to the house and played whist for a while. Mary was still exhausted, so she went to bed early. Henry followed shortly. He didn't want to be to far from her at any time. He heard Mary go to bed and he went into his room to read for a while.

Henry dozed off for maybe two hours. When he awoke, he heard someone moving around. He ran to the door and opened it, there was a figure of a person going to the third floor. Henry followed, but saw no trace of anyone upstairs. He came downstairs and listened at Mary's door for a few minutes. He heard her moving around, so he knew it wasn't her that went up the stairs. Henry searched the house before going back to bed but found nothing.

Henry planned to check out the house more thoroughly in the light of day. He knew he saw someone or something, but couldn't figure out how they entered the house. Everything was locked up tight. Henry would not tell the women about tonight, he was afraid it would upset them. But he would go through the house from attic to basement to check for secret entrances. He fell into a light sleep at around four a.m. Henry kept wondering who was trying to frighten Mary off the island and why?

Everyone was up bright and early next morning, Mathew and Henry were about finished with the stables. Henry had been on the island for four days and he was terribly worried.

Mary looked cheerful this morning she was excited about the horses coming in three days. She could hardly wait. Mary wanted to ride all over her island and inspect every inch of it. She was happy for the first time in months. Henry was here, Pris was with her and she owned this island, and horses to boot. Mary couldn't think of anything else that could have made her any happier.

Mary was going to the stables today with Henry and Mathew. She enjoyed being around the two men, Mathew was a father figure to her. She was very fond of Mathew and he took to her immediately.

Mathew was a kind, gentle man, who knew the ladies were in trouble and he intended to stay pretty close to them. His family was a long way away, he became very fond of Mary and her aunt. Mathew was told of the strange things that were haunting Mary and he vowed to let nothing harm her.

All three arrived at the stables before nine o'clock and went to work to put the finishing touches on it. Mary painted the trim, and around the doors and stalls. Henry and Mary played around most of the morning. Mathew thought they acted like two love birds chasing each other around the stalls splattering paint on each other. Mathew liked seeing her so relaxed and worry free.

Mathew hoped since Henry was here that she wouldn't have anymore bad nights. He just didn't know that more was in store for her than ever before. Work was halted around one thirty p.m. and they went to the house for a light lunch.

Mary went up to change and found her door open. She opened the door and let out a scream. Mary fainted, when she came too all she remembered was a woman in a veil standing in the middle of her room.

Henry and Mathew ran upstairs in a hurry to Mary's room. She was lying on the floor just outside her door. Henry picked her up, and carried her to the bed and laid her down gently. He sent Mathew after the smelling salts, and Pris.

Mary came to and sat up looking horrified. "Henry, where did the young woman go and how did she get here?"

"I know I've seen her somewhere, but I can't place it. She scared the life out of me. I never expected to find someone in here when I opened the door. I'm sorry I shouldn't be so fragile or jumpy. I guess these last few months have really taken a toll on me."

Henry asked if she was alright. After Mary told him she was fine. He went in search of the woman Mary had seen in her room. She did not come down the stairs, so she must have gone upstairs. Henry searched the third floor, the attic and found nothing. He joined Mathew and Pris in Mary's room. They thought it was a good idea for Mary to rest for the remainder of the day. Pris brought Mary a light supper and sat with her for a while. Mary was still upset over the young woman that was in her room. She knew she recognized her from somewhere. Pris suggested Mary take something to help her rest, and try to forget about the afternoon.

Henry stopped in to say goodnight and to wish her a restful night. Henry intended to search the house again before going to bed. He went up to the third floor and searched each room, he wanted to tap on the walls but was afraid of disturbing Mary. He would test the walls tomorrow.

The house was locked up so Henry went up and prepared for bed. Everything was quite for the rest of the night. Henry was awake early, he was looking forward to the arrival of the horses.

Mary stayed in bed most of the day resting. She wanted to meet the boat when it arrived with her horses. Henry spent the morning tapping on walls but found nothing unusual. By the time Henry came down Mary was up and stirring about.

They ate lunch together and went to the dock to await the boat from Pineda. They were all excited about the arrival of the stud and mare. The male horse was solid white, and the mare was black as night. Mary knew they were the most beautiful horses she'd ever seen and they were from good stock. Mary chose the stud and named him Lighting. Pris took the black mare and named her Thunder. Mathew took the horses to there new home. The ladies returned to the house, they would give the horses time to settle in and rest before attempting to ride them. It was a hot breezy day, the kind of day you would just lounge around the house and keep cool in any way you could.

Everyone sat on the patio drinking lemonade Sara made earlier that day. Mary wanted to go for a swim, but just couldn't get up the energy to go. So she decided on a cool bath before bedtime. They discussed plans for the following day, if the horses were settled in they would take a ride around the island. Pris was more than happy to let Henry ride her mare. Pris knew Mary would be safer with Henry along. After dinner everyone played whist until eleven thirty and Pris told Mary she ought to go to bed.

"Alright, Pris. I know I will be up early in the morning getting ready for our picnic." Mary went to her room and got ready for bed. She took a cool bath which helped relax her. She went to bed and slept that night. Mary was up early next morning fixing a picnic basket for herself and Henry. She packed fried chicken that was in the ice box, sweet potato yams, bread, green beans, and apple pie.

Henry came downstairs looking for her. Mary told him she wanted to go to the sacrifice altar and look around today. Henry saw no harm in going there, but he didn't know about Mary's dream of the place. They left for the stables around eight o'clock to saddle the horses for their ride. It looked as if they would have a beautiful day. Mary kept thinking about the altar that haunted her dreams at night. Something kept pulling at her to go the altar. It was as if she were reliving a bad dream.

They arrived at the altar about an hour later, Mary dismounted and went up to the altar to have a look. When she touched the altar she remembered a night long ago. She shivered and Henry asked her if she was cold. "No, Henry I just got a strange feeling. I feel like I've been here before in another time."

Henry looked puzzled. He really was worried about her now. "Mary, lets find another spot for our picnic, all of a sudden I don't think we need to be here."

"Alright, Henry, I would feel better some place else too." They went farther into the woods and found a lovely clearing. "I think this is perfect, Henry, do you like it?"

"Yes I do, its beautiful." They spread a blanket on the ground and laid out the food Mary prepared for them. After lunch they just relaxed and lounged on the blanket after the food was put away. Henry knew he was falling hopelessly in love with Mary. He knew he couldn't leave her now. It was getting late and Henry told Mary they needed to get back.

Pris and Mathew were waiting for them to return. Mathew took the horses to the stable and brushed them down. He told Henry and Mary he'd join them later. Dinner was ready for the family after they freshened up.

Mary retired early that evening, she was very tired. She was asleep for about two hours when she began to dream of the altar and the unknown girl. She could see Barnamus at the altar with the young woman. He was holding a knife above her. The girl began to scream. Henry woke Mary from her dream. Mary looked at Henry and flung herself into his arms "Mary, what were you screaming about, I heard you down in the parlor. You scared me half to death. You look as if you've seen a ghost." Mary proceeded to tell Henry of her dream. "Henry, I'm the girl in my dreams. I know it sounds crazy, but I lived in that time with Barnamus Hillard. Henry, I'm frightened. Please stay with me for the rest of the night. Maybe I'm going crazy like my mother did." Henry told her he wouldn't allow that to happen to her. He'd protect her from whatever was happening on this island.

He was more determined now than ever to find out what was going on here. Mary lay back down and Henry positioned himself in a chair by the window. Mary tossed and mumbled in her sleep. The moon was bright that night, and while he was looking out the window he saw the creature looking up at Mary's window. He couldn't leave her to follow whatever or whoever was looking at Mary's window.

Henry decided to place Mathew outside to stand guard the next night. In the wee hours of the morning he dozed off. He woke before Mary and let her sleep late. The night had been a restless one for her. He left her door open so he could hear and went to his room to freshen up. "When Mary wakes I will go look for tracks," he thought. Mary woke up around nine in the morning. Henry took this opportunity to go see if there were tracks left by the visitor last night. Henry searched the grounds thoroughly, but found nothing.

He returned to the house and ate breakfast. After he finished he went to find Mathew to tell him of the creature he'd seen last night. Mathew promised to keep an eye on the house that night. Henry would not let the women wonder far from the house alone until he found some answers. He would have his hands full with Mary. She loved to roam the island.

He was going to take the door off the hinges and see what was in that locked room that fascinated Mary so. Maybe there would be an answer there, he'd see. Henry went to the cellar to get some tools to work with. Mary was thrilled to know that finally she was going to be able to see inside that locked room. Henry pried and pried on the hinges, "This door was built to last Mary." The top hinge finally let go, there were just two more to go. He didn't expect to find much in the room, but he needed to know.

When the door was finally down he and Mary entered the room together. The room was very clean no dust anywhere. The closet was filled with beautiful gowns and a slight smell of honeysuckle could be detected. There was water in the washbasin. Mary was very puzzled now. The room was locked, but it appeared someone was living here. There must be another way into this room. They looked under the bed, and tapped the walls, looked in the closet . Behind the clothes in the closet they found a hidden staircase, going up stairs and down stairs. Henry went for a lantern. He was going to follow the stairs to see where they lead. At the end of the stairs was a tunnel; he followed the path, which didn't appear to have been used in a very long time. He came out next to the altar where Barnamus sacrificed humans to his God. He tried to close off the tunnel as well as he could. Then Henry went back to the house to tell Mary where the tunnel led.

"I'm going to stay in that room tonight, and see what happens."

Mary wanted to join him, but he refused to let her stay.

"I don't know what I'll find in there tonight, and I don't want you to be there you might get hurt."

"Then do be careful Henry. I won't sleep any tonight worrying about you." After dinner Henry settled down in the locked room for the night. The moon was shinning very bright he could see the entire room.

Around midnight he was aroused by a noise, he must have drifted off to sleep. He saw a beautiful young woman standing near the dresser, she was watching him. She lifted her arm and pointed at him and said, "Leave Singer Island before it's too late." And then she vanished before his eyes. There was the strong smell of honeysuckle in the room. Henry rubbed his eyes, surely he must have been dreaming. But the smell of honeysuckle was real, very real. Henry didn't figure he'd see or hear anything more that night, so he went to bed.

Henry awoke early the next morning and lay in bed to think about the visitor from last night. He wanted to believe that he was dreaming, but down deep inside he knew he wasn't. She was a very beautiful woman, and she looked like someone he knew. He got up and dressed and went down in search of a cup of coffee. Maybe that would clear his head.

Pris was sitting at the table, he told her of the visit from the lady and what she told him. Priscilla did not know why the house was being haunted. When Mary walked into the dinning room, Henry looked as if he just saw a ghost. Priscilla asked Henry if he was alright?

"Yes, I know who the woman was that I saw last night."

"What woman, Henry?" asked Mary.

So Henry proceeded to tell Mary about the woman.

"Oh, Henry! I'm frightened, I knew I saw a woman upstairs. Who was she Henry?"

"She was your mother Mary."

Mary passed out in a cold faint on to the floor. Henry carried her to the sofa and got the smelling salts to bring her around.

Mary looked so pale and helpless, Henry's heart went out to her. When Mary came too, Henry told her of her mother's warning.

"I can't leave here yet, Henry there's so much I don't understand."

Henry felt the same way, but he was worried about Mary.

CHAPTER ELEVEN

Mary wanted to stay in the room tonight with Henry. So Henry agreed to let her stay. Maybe Beth Windsor would talk to her daughter. After dinner Henry and Mary went to the room to settle down for the night. Mary was scared beyond belief, but she would face whatever it was that haunted that room. Around one a.m. again the scent of honeysuckle could be detected. Mary waited patiently for her mother or the ghostly appearance of something. Nothing happened except the smell of honeysuckle. Mary drifted off to sleep.

Mary felt a hand on her shoulder and jerked upright. Her mother stood beside her. Mary gasped.

"Don't be afraid my darling. I have been with you since your birth. I vowed not to let what happened to me, happen to you. Dear, I know you've seen him twice, but he didn't harm you. Remember the dream you had of Barnamus hanging, the girl you saw in the bushes was you, in another time. You were the only one he ever truly loved. And dear, sweet Pris I knew she was a good woman she has taken such good care of you. I couldn't have done any better myself. I didn't want to die, but the power was stronger than I was. I hated leaving your father. You must move out of the room your in. That was my room and it seems that the power is stronger there. It must have been Barnamus' room. You need to get strong so you can keep your sanity."

Mary promised her mother she would be careful. Mary was more at peace than she'd been in a long time. The presence of her mother was very comforting. Beth was truly a beautiful woman.

Henry had been asleep through all of this, but he saw Mary was at peace. "Your mother was here, wasn't she Mary?"

"Yes, Henry, and she told me a lot about the creature we've been seeing here. It's Barnamus wanting revenge; he doesn't want any of you here. He's after me because I was the one he was in love with so many years ago. Mother told me you need to be very careful, he's jealous of us. She also wants me to move out of that room, it was her room and it also belonged to Barnamus. Mother thinks the power is stronger in that room. I told her I would move to another room in the morning."

Mary and Henry went to her room to wait till morning; it would be another long night. They couldn't wait till the sun came up. Nights were a dreaded time in the Windsor household.

Mary awoke to find Henry sleeping in a chair by the window. She lay there watching him sleep she realized how much she loved him already. Mary knew Henry would protect her from whatever her mother was warning her about. Mary was very frightened but she couldn't leave.

Mary still couldn't tell Pris about the visit from her mother. She knew it would upset her so she kept it to herself. Mary needed time to think before Pris found out anything. Poor Henry was worried enough for the both of them. Mary was determined to speak to the creature now, even though her mother warned against her being alone with it. She hoped it could talk. Maybe she could find answers to a lot of questions about things that were happening on the island. She would sneak away from Henry and Pris somehow and see what she could find out.

Henry awoke and smiled at Mary. "You look beautiful even when you awake in the morning."

"Your not so bad yourself. Are you ready for breakfast?"

"To tell you the truth I need coffee more than anything else."

"Well go wash up and meet me in the kitchen in ten minutes. I'll fix you some eggs, bacon, biscuits, and coffee."

"That sounds good, you have a deal."

Mary got up and combed her long blonde hair, then quickly dressed. She noticed a lot of her mother's features in her face.

She thought her father a very lucky man to have found her mother. Since talking with her mother Mary felt better, more like her old self. She would find out what was happening here one way or another.

Henry was already down stairs when Mary came down. He helped with breakfast, all the time watching Mary. Mary seemed different, more like the woman he met on the boat months ago. Henry couldn't let anything happen to Mary, she was his destiny. He never thought of himself as being one to be tied down, Mary changed that thought in him. Henry asked Mary if she would like to go riding this morning.

Mary said she would love to, she wanted to see if she could find the creature but she wouldn't let Henry know that was the reason she wanted to go. And if she saw it, she'd find a way to follow it and try to talk with the beast. After breakfast she went upstairs to change into her ridding clothes. She met Henry in the hall and they went to the stables.

Mathew was cleaning the stables. He told Mary it was a beautiful morning for a ride. Henry and Mathew saddled the horses while Mary looked around the barn. As soon as the horses were saddled they were ready to leave for a ride down the beach. They rode through the waves that rushed onto the beach. After playing for awhile Mary headed for the altar. Henry asked if she really wanted to go there again. "I have to face it sometime or be frightened forever."

They rode for quite a while and Mary decided to stop and rest. They were dismounting when Mary saw the creature again, she yelled for it to stop, but it seemed scared and kept on going. Mary told Henry she wanted to try to speak with the being.

"That might be too dangerous Mary. You don't know what it might do, it is a wild animal you know."

"I just don't think it will hurt me. It had a chance the first night we were here. It turned and ran. I don't know why it is here, but I don't think it means me any harm." Henry was worried now since he knew Mary's intentions to speak with whatever that thing was. Henry would really have to watch Mary now because he knew her well enough to know that when she set her mind to do something she would do it one way or another. "Mary are you ready to go back? I have a few things I need to do."

"Yes, there's no reason to stay out here any longer. I doubt it will come back today."

They rode back in silence. Henry wondering all the way what Mary was thinking. He would talk to Pris and tell her about the past few days. Pris would really be shocked. Henry couldn't handle it alone, he needed all the help he could get with Mary now.

Mathew was nowhere in sight when they returned, so Henry groomed the horses and fed them before they went to the house. When they got to the house Mary went upstairs to change and freshen up, and Henry went in search of Pris. "I think you better sit down, I have some unbelievable news."

Pris sat down and listened to Henry's story of her sister-in-law's visit to Mary and of the warning of the creature. Pris just couldn't believe what she was hearing. It must be a bad dream, all the things he was telling her just couldn't be true. It was impossible, but it was happening, her dead sister-in-law was talking to her niece. "Henry, we have got to get her off this Island before something dreadful happens to her. Her poor mother died a horrible death, because we didn't believe her. If only we would have taken the time and listened, she would be alive today. I know Mary can be very stubborn, but we have to convince her to go. She loves you, maybe she will listen to you."

Henry thought he could at least try, so he went in search of Mary to ask her to leave the Island she loved so much. He found her upstairs looking out over the grounds toward the woods.

"Mary, I would like to talk to you about something very important."

"Alright, Henry, what is it?"

"I would like for you to leave this place with me today. It is getting very dangerous here for you and I can't stand by and watch you get hurt. Please do this for me and Pris you have her worried sick."

"I can't do that Henry, I have to find out what's going on here, not just for myself but for my mother as well. Something killed her and I intend to find out who or what it was."

"I'm sorry you feel that way Mary. But I will try to understand for your sake. Is there anything I can do to help?"

"No just stand by me and give me hope."

"Alright, lets figure out a way to find this thing you want to talk to. We need to trap it, set some kind of snare or dig a hole to catch it. We need to have it penned up so it won't be dangerous to you. I'll talk to Mathew and set up a plan with him." Henry left to find Mathew and tell him of his and Mary's plan. They could use some of the old traps they found to place around the island, and check them everyday. They would catch this thing that was running loose here one way or another. Henry found Mathew and they got to work fixing the traps and placed them around the house in the woods.

Henry would check them before going to bed and see what he caught. He really hoped nothing, because he didn't know what that thing was capable of. He knew it would be angry when caught in one of the traps and he didn't want to tangle with it. He wondered what they were going to do with it when and if it was caught. Oh well, he'd deal with that when the time came. Henry checked the trap before going to bed and found nothing. This creature was very smart, he could see where it circled around the trap and then went on its way. It would be challenging to catch it. Henry told Mary the traps were empty, but he didn't tell her the creature had been there and circled the trap. He couldn't tell her they were dealing with something that was intelligent.

Henry would devise another plan, it was like the creature knew what was planned. Maybe Mary's mother was right and that scared the devil out of him.

Henry just wanted Mary to be safe. That night Henry heard the horrifying howling of the creature they pursued. He wondered if they had finally caught it. Henry really hoped not, for he did not know what he would do with it after they caught it. He checked in on Mary to see if she was sleeping. She seemed to be resting for now. Henry returned to his room to fall into a deep sleep, he was exhausted from sitting up most nights watching Mary.

Next morning, he went to check on the traps and in the last one he encountered the creature face to face. "Oh God, how horrible it looks," he thought. He didn't know what to do.

He went in search of Mathew. After telling him of his catch they went looking for chains. If they could get close enough they would chain him before they removed the trap. Henry needed a place for the creature after they chained him. He thought about the cabin that was falling down on the middle of the island. Henry wanted to try to communicate with it before Mary knew he captured it.

The creature was very angry, so that made it hard to chain it, they finally wore it down and managed to get it in chains. It watched every move Henry and Mathew made. Henry kept reassuring it that they did not want to hurt it, they just wanted to try to talk with him. The creature seemed to understand everything Henry was saying to him. He got calm, finally. The thing seemed to have a lot of sense.

Henry tried to communicate, but it was useless. The creature couldn't speak. Henry would look for another way to try to find out who this was, and why it was here, how long it had been here. Maybe it would respond better to Mary. He would tell her now because he couldn't find a way to reach this creature.

Henry was very tired after the struggle of getting that wild animal to the cabin. After making sure everything was secure Henry went to the house for a while. Whatever was locked up in that building made him feel as if it could read his mind. He made sure there was water for the being before he left it to calm down. Mary was in the sitting room when Henry got to the house. Mary was very inquisitive about Henry's morning.

"Mary we have it chained up in the old cabin for now, we're waiting for it to calm down some. I have never seen such a strong being in all my life. It took all Mathew and I could do to get it in chains and to the cabin.

"I tried to communicate with it, but it was useless. I thought maybe after it calms down maybe you could give it a try, it seems fascinated by you for some reason."

"I hope you didn't hurt him, Henry. I bet he was scared to death being put in chains after being free. He was here first we invaded his territory by coming here. I would love to know how he got on this island. He's probably the only one who knows what's truly going on here on the island and he can't tell us at this point. I know my mother warned me about it, but I feel a closeness I can't explain."

Mary and Henry went to the cabin where the being was chained and Mary tried to talk to it. "We won't hurt you. I just want to talk to you. You see there have been some very strange happenings in the house since I arrived. It terrifies me since I learned the history of my ancestors. It seems they were believed to have gone crazy, but I believe something truly scared them to death." The creature kept his eyes on Mary, it seemed as if he understood her. Mary would teach him to talk and then he could tell her what she wanted to know. It appeared that the answers lay with him.

It would take time but Mary felt it would be worth the effort. Keeping him calm would be a task but they were afraid to unchain him at the present. They didn't even know what his food source was, or anything else for that matter. He was used to being free and fending for himself. If only they knew he ate what they ate. Sara had been sneaking him food for a long time. They brought him wild berries, roots and herbs, but he wouldn't touch them. "Henry, we can't let him starve to death."

Mary spent a lot of time with him trying to teach him to communicate. It would certainly be a challenge to teach this being anything. Mary told Pris about the capture of the creature and she was horrified. "Mary it's not right to cage something up that is wild. I worry about you getting hurt."

Sara overheard the conversation and knew that she must free him as soon as possible. She would have to watch for the perfect time. But for now she must feed him. She knew it would be too dangerous for them to learn the whole truth about the island. Sara wished a thousand times she didn't know of the horrible things that happened here. But she promised to take care of the one called Luke, the one they had locked away.

A long time ago she promised Mr. Windsor to look after the thing that was running loose on the island. He had known the truth about it ever since Mr. Windsor's grandfather agreed to buy the island from the Hillards. They took care of it since the hanging of Barnamus Hillard. It was very old and he took care of it down through the years. Now Sara was responsible for it.

Mary kept everyone away from it as much as possible. Mary didn't know Sara was feeding it when no one was around. Mary worked every day with the creature to no avail. She just knew that sooner or later it would talk to her and tell her the things she wanted to know.

He watched her with every move she made. It was as if he knew just what she was thinking. She got up to leave for the day and he made a motion for her to stay. "I have to go now. It's almost dinner." He made a motion with his hand as if to eat. "Yes, its time to eat."

Mary decided to bring some food from the house to him. This was a step in the right direction. He understood it was time to eat and she knew now that she could teach him. Mary couldn't wait to tell Henry of the progress she made today.

Pris was in the parlor waiting for Mary, wanting to hear of her efforts with the being. "Please, be very careful, Mary, he may be testing you. He might be smarter than any of us give him credit. You know what your mother told you about him."

"I will, Pris. I just need to get him to understand what I need to know from him and then I will be happy to turn him loose again. If that's what he wants. If only I could get him to communicate, there would be no reason for him to go back living like he was. I don't know why he looks like he does, but we have a place for him to stay. No one will ever have to know about him at all. We will take care of him for the rest of his life."

Mary went in search of Henry to tell him that the creature understood her when she got ready to leave for dinner. "He really understood, he made a motion with his hand to eat. I don't feel so afraid of him anymore. I think in time he could be very gentle. I wish we didn't have to keep him locked up, but I guess its best for now. At least, until we know he won't hurt us and he knows we won't hurt him. Henry, go with me to feed him. I want you to see how he acts with me, it's as if he cares for me."

That really scared Henry for the warning from Mary's mother to stay away from this being, because it was controlled from beyond the grave by Barnamus. What evils had Barnamus unveiled? Was he capable of returning from the beyond to fulfill his threat? Henry could not say. He believed in God and he guessed Satan as well. He guessed it was possible for evil to prevail. This was the part he was unsure about. Heaven help them if it were true. They didn't have a chance against the forces of evil. Henry agreed to go with Mary. It was getting dark and he didn't want her out alone even if the thing was locked up. Henry's feelings were that nothing could hold this being if he chose not to be held.

When Mary and Henry got to the cabin the creature was crouched in a corner and wouldn't approach them. "He must be frightened of you Henry, you were one of the ones who put him here. I can't really blame him for being frightened of you, if you chained me, I'd be afraid too. He is really very different with me.

"I will teach him to talk and then you will see the change for yourself. I told Pris we would keep him here on the island and take care of him . No one need know anything about him. I won't allow people to see him and think he is a freak of nature and make fun of him. I will protect him from that at any cost. He is human, even if he does look like a beast."

"Lets go back to the house Mary it's getting late."

Mary was suddenly very tired as if her life was being drained from her. The creature was staring intensely at her. Henry noticed the change immediately and knew the creature in some way was responsible for Mary's lack of energy. Henry quickly escorted her outside from the prying eyes of their guest. Mary recovered shortly and told Henry she was fine. I don't know what came over me, but all of a sudden I could barely move. She was aware they needed to get back to the house. Pris would be worried. Mary was delusional about that thing that was locked up in the cabin. How could she possibly think they could communicate with each other? Here she was wanting to dress it in clothes and make it appear he was just like anyone else.

Henry could not see this happening. Mary needed to find some clothes for him. She wondered if she could get him to put them on.

CHAPTER TWELVE

Mary would go to the attic in the morning and find some things of her grand-fathers for him to wear, but now she wanted to go home eat and fall into bed. Mary couldn't figure out why she was so tired all of a sudden. Henry walked Mary to the house, changed for dinner and met her back in the dinning room. Henry could tell Mary's mind was somewhere else. She wasn't herself tonight. He would make sure she got some rest.

Mary was up early next morning looking in the attic for clothes for her friend. Why she thought he was her friend was beyond her. But she felt a kinship with him. Henry and Pris thought she was out of her mind if she thought she was going to get clothes on him. "Pris, it's worth a try, he can't run around in animal hides forever."

Henry thought it would take more than Mary to get clothes on it, more like a miracle. But Henry would do whatever he could to help Mary.

Sara was in the kitchen fixing food for him, he had never hurt her in all the years she cared for it, but since it was chained she didn't know what he might do. Sara still remembered the day she first laid eyes on him, she was only eleven. It scared her half to death. She went running to Mr. Windsor crying like the devil himself was after her.

Mr. Windsor told her not to be afraid, it wouldn't hurt her. He explained about the curse the witch put on the Hillard family after they bought Singer Island. Barnamus mother was with child and when the child was born it was covered with hair and looked and sounded very much like an animal. Everyone was repulsed it was horrid looking. It brought shame to the family. The whole town was alive with gossip, wondering what had Lady Hillard done to give birth to such a being. It was rumored she made a pact with the devil and didn't keep her promise. People were so superstitious back then. If they couldn't explain it the only explanation was witch craft or Satan. No one could take care of it so it was left at the cliffs to die, but it survived and ran loose on the island terrifying everyone in its path. This creature was Barnamus brother. The midwife told Barnamus mother the baby died during birth. She did not want anyone seeing what she'd seen. She took the thing to the cliffs and left it there to die or be eaten by the wild animals. She dared not kill it for if it were truly born from evil, she did not want anything to happen to her family. At this point she was terrified. Did she do the right thing? Mr. Hillard would have been furious if he saw what he helped create. He would surely have blamed his wife. To him nothing was ever his fault.

Barnamus came upon the tiny bundle while out walking along the cliffs. He did not know it was his brother. Only that it was little and needed caring for. It was ugly, there was hair from its head to its feet. But the facial features were of a person. Whatever it was Barnamus would care for it.

Barnamus was only eight years old himself and knew nothing about feeding an infant. But Barnamus knew it needed milk, so he left the infant near a den of wild dogs. Hoping they would feed it. The dogs circled around the bundle sniffing cautiously. There was a lot of growling and snarling between the dogs.

A female emerged from the den smelled around the bundle, pulled the blanket off and gently nudged the small hairy creature with her nose. She proceeded to wash it, then picked it up gently in her mouth and carried it inside the den with her.

Barnamus knew she would feed it. He would from this point on keep a close watch over his friend. He felt a bond between them. For the rest of Barnamus life he watched the little fellow grow up from a distance. It was as if, at times, it knew Barnamus was near.

He would sniff the air and catch a familiar scent. He saw Barnamus around quite often. Over the years he got brave enough to come within a few hundred yards of Barnamus. His pack would not attempt this, but there was a stirring inside that he could not explain.

From the time he could walk on all fours he would slip away from the pack and watch the humans. He listened to their language, watched them walk, heard their laughter, he felt so confused. Deep within himself he felt drawn to these humans.

After awhile he tried imitating the sounds he heard and found he could make them also. Why couldn't the pack make these noises? As he managed to make more and more of the sounds the pack pulled away from him.

They feared human sounds. So he was left to his own resources and felt more compelled to learn about this new animal he had encountered since his birth. To him these were just another species he knew nothing about.

So over the course of years he learned to imitate the language. He just didn't know what the words meant. He would walk around for hours just repeating what he'd heard and was clueless to the meaning. This is how Barnamus discovered he could talk.

Barnamus was strolling along the cliffs aimlessly, when he heard someone talking. He wondered who it could be. He went in search of the voice. Barnamus was amazed to find it was the creature talking to himself.

Barnamus didn't want to frighten him so he sat down a short distance away and listened until he was spotted. Barnamus quietly held up one hand and spoke gently. "Do not be afraid, I won't hurt you."

It just stood there looking at Barnamus with a puzzled expression on its face. Barnamus continued to speak slow and easy to it. After many days of talking to him, the creature relaxed enough to get closer. Barnamus began to teach it what words meant. Barnamus would use objects to teach him what the words meant.

It was easy with food, he liked to eat and was eager to try whatever Barnamus offered. Some things he liked and some things he didn't. Soon it became apparent that he depended on Barnamus for his food supply.

Barnamus kept him a secret from everyone at the house. He decided he needed to name him. So he called him Luke. Barnamus would hear tales sometimes of some spotting the creature around the island. He would immediately poke fun at the person and the wild imagination he possessed.

He would tell them of the hours spent roaming around the island and tell them he never saw such a being as they were describing. He would remind them he'd been on this island his whole life and covered every inch of it. And nothing by that description ever crossed his path. Barnamus did not want people knowing of his friend. He was afraid they would try to kill Luke. These people were after all very superstitious. If something could not be explained it must be witchcraft.

CHAPTER THIRTEEN

The whole town of Pineda thought Barnamus was strange. He hardly joined the activities. They saw him as a recluse. Wild stories started flying around about him worshiping the devil. Some one said they passed close by where he was and heard other voices, but did not see another person.

The stories started about the baby the devil had spawned with Mrs. Hillard and that Barnamus was probably a vessel that was being used to protect the creature. Over the course of time the stories became wilder to the point Barnamus was supposed to be sacrificing humans at an alter built at the center of the island.

Barnamus met and fell in love with a girl from Brunswick, Georgia. He met her while he was on business at St. Simons Island. Over the weeks he was there they spent every spare moment together.

He convinced Maria's parents to let her accompany him back to his Island, to meet his parents. They were to be married in a month. Maria was beautiful, with a passion for life and adventure. Maria loved the Island as much as Barnamus. They roamed the entire island, Maria came to know it as well as he did.

Barnamus took Maria to meet his friend after swearing her to secrecy. Maria was amazed at this person who spoke as they spoke, but looked like a hideous monster. She was not frightened by him though. She felt a gentleness from him especially towards Barnamus.

Everyone was joyous over the impending wedding. A week before Maria was to become his bride, she was walking along the cliffs and slipped and fell to her death. Barnamus could not catch her in time. Maria was swept out into the ocean. Her body was never recovered.

Barnamus was devastated, he became recluse wandering the shores at night looking for Maria. It was at this point the stories started again about Barnamus sacrificing young women on the altar.

After Maria's death he was rarely seen, he forbade anyone to come to the Island except Sara's grandfather. Lester Bunt brought supplies to Barnamus every week. Lester knew of the half human man, but said nothing to Barnamus about it.

Lester never told a soul, not even his family. He respected Barnamus privacy. He figured the man was suffering enough.

One stormy night the townpeople got in an uproar. One of the young women from town was missing. They never suspected she'd run off with someone.

Talk started about Barnamus and tempers flared. They got into their boats and went to the island. They seized Barnamus and dragged him to the alter at the center of the island. Nobody would listen to his pleas or answer his questions. They hung him in a horrid fashion. His friend was unable to help him, there were too many of them. Luke was frightened so bad he ran as fast as he could away from the scene. This was the last day Luke spoke to anyone, not even to himself.

He would never forget what these humans did to the only one that ever loved him.

He really took to Barnamus, after his death he howled for days, it drove Mrs. Hillard mad. From then on the women started loosing their minds. It was very sad.

Sara really felt sorry for Pris and Mary. She could already see the changes in Mary just in the past few months. She was too lovely and sweet to go through something like this, but she was a true Windsor stubborn to a fault.

Sara just hoped what happened to both Mrs. Windsors didn't happen to Mary or Pris. All women that owned the island were cursed if they chose to live here. Sara couldn't bring herself to tell anyone what she knew, so she finished what she was doing and slipped away into the night to feed her friend of so many years. When she arrived she found him already eating. "Well, at least they've found out what you eat. I will check on you every day, don't worry Mary will never let anyone harm you. She is a very loving woman. She only wants to know what's going on here and what happened to her mother and grandmother. You must promise not to harm her in any way." He looked at Sara and only shook his head. He understood all right if Mary only knew how much he did understand.

Sara went back to the house and cleared the table. They were finished with their meal, so Sara served coffee in the parlor for everyone. "Where were you? We looked but couldn't find you?"

"I went out for some fresh air. It gets so hot in the kitchen standing over that stove."

Mary was very suspicious of Sara since she pulled that disappearing act a few weeks ago. But Mary said nothing at the time. Mary would watch and follow her some time just to see where she was going. But for now Mary had other things on her mind like clothes for her friend. She couldn't keep calling him a creature. He needed a name. For some reason she felt responsible for him. He didn't frighten her as much anymore. She looked forward to the day she could turn him loose and be able to trust him. She found a lot of clothes in the trunks, but none that looked like they would fit.

CHAPTER FOURTEEN

Mary needed a name for her friend, but nothing seemed to fit so far. He seemed to notice when Mary entered. This was a good sign she believed. Luke thought she was Maria the one from long ago who Barnamus loved so much. Mary looked just like Maria. Luke remembered how sweet and kind she was to him and how much time they spent together.

Luke promised Sara that he wouldn't hurt anyone, but he needed to be free. He was chained to the wall like an animal. His appearance might fit the part, but his heart was a far cry from being that.

He had feelings, thoughts just like anyone else. Just because he chose not to express them didn't mean they were not real. Luke witnessed the horrors of horrors at the hand of people the night his friend was killed.

So even though he promised not to hurt anyone it remained a struggle to continue to be chained like this. Luke never lived inside. He could feel the walls closing in. He became exceedingly restless. On Sara's visits she could tell he was getting to the point where he could not contain himself.

Sara could take it no longer. That night after everyone was asleep she crept quietly from the house. Sara got to the cabin looked around so as not to be detected and slipped inside. Luke was huddled in the corner looking helpless.

Sara went over to Luke and whispered, "I'm here to set you free, I can't stand watching you be chained anymore. Stay out of sight. I will feed you as I have done for years. I know your drawn to Mary but stay away please."

Luke looked up at her and nodded. Sara released Luke back into the wild. Luke was glad to be free, he ran for miles along the beach feeling every muscle in his body cramping. He had not exercised in weeks since being locked in the cabin. It felt good running with the wind, to hear the night come alive with sounds he was so familiar with since birth.

Sara returned to the house undetected. She felt better about Luke being free. It's true he looked horrid but no one should be treated as Luke was treated.

Next morning everyone was up early. Mary was always eager to go see her friend every morning. She ate breakfast hurriedly and fixed some to carry with her and was out the door. Mary enjoyed the sun. The breeze was always blowing in off the ocean. The days were not as blistery hot now as they were a few months ago. She liked this time of year.

Mary was at the cabin when she noticed the door was open. She ran the rest of the way in a panic. Afraid for her friend. How did the door get opened? As she stepped inside she realized her friend was gone. In the corner lay the chains that he was wearing yesterday. How did he manage to get out of them?

Mary was heart broken that he was gone. She had made plans for him. Where could he be. She knew he was some where on the island, but this was a big place. He could stay hidden for a long time before he was seen again.

Luke knew the island better than anyone. After all he did grow up here, evading people for years and years.

Mary returned to the house and told everyone that her friend was gone. Pris could see the sadness in Mary's face. Henry for one was glad he'd gone. But now there was another concern. Would he be watching Mary from some hidden spot?

Mary wondered around the house. She could not believe he was gone. Mary thought she had made some progress with him in the two weeks he'd been at the cabin. She would not give up the idea that he might come back or that she would see him again.

The days passed and Mary slowly became withdrawn again. She was staying more to herself. Now that she was staying in more, she started seeing the woman again and hearing voices. Mary moved out of her mothers bedroom, but the dreams still occurred.

Now her friend was a part of her dreams, as well as Barnamus. She knew she loved him and was very fond of his friend Luke who looked like her friend here. But his name in her dream was Luke. And the woman looked like her, but her name was Maria.

In Mary's dream she could see Barnamus, Maria, and Luke talking and walking along the cliffs. They seemed to be very happy.

Somewhere the dream took a turn and there was a sadness that was unbearable. She saw Maria slip and fall from the cliff. Barnamus tried to catch her but couldn't. Her body was washed out by the current in the ocean.

Mary could see Barnamus standing on the cliff, he was screaming and Luke was running around in circles not knowing what to do.

Mary awoke with great sadness. It was crushing her. What horror had her friend lived through. No wonder he lived in exile. She must find him. Was the recognition in his eyes because he thought she was Maria?

When Mary dressed she went for some coffee and biscuits. She thought of Luke, yes this was what she would call him it just felt right.

Was Luke hungry, cold? She needed to know. She ate hurriedly and wrapped a few biscuits in a napkin and was out the door. She didn't care how long it took, she'd find Luke and help him. Now she knew how.

CHAPTER FIFTEEN

Mary checked the cabin just to be sure he was not there. The cabin stood empty, as before. Mathew was at the stables and she asked if he'd saddle her horse for her.

"Mary, are you sure you'll be safe out ridding alone. That thing is probably mad and might try to hurt you."

"Mathew I don't believe he will, he knows me from another time. But he knew me as Maria, not Mary.

"Mary, what are you talking about?"

"I was here when Barnamus was alive. I knew him and Luke."

Mathew was scared. He'd never heard Mary tell such nonsense. But he kept listening.

Mary was hoping he'd hurry with her horse. She needed to be on her way. "Mathew, I saw us in a dream playing along the cliffs, Barnamus, Luke and myself. That's why he's so fascinated with me, he thinks I'm Maria."

Mathew finished saddling the horse and told Mary to be careful. Mary promised she would.

Mathew hurried to the main house to tell Henry and Pris what Mary told him and that she was riding looking for the creature she named Luke.

Henry told Pris he would ride out and look for Mary. She was certainly headed for a breakdown. Henry was sure of it. Such wild stories she was telling him.

Mary was almost to the altar when movement caught her eye. She thought for a moment she saw Barnamus. But this could not be true. Barnamus was dead. Buried in the cemetery not to far from here. Her eyes were playing tricks on her.

She would continue to search for Luke, he must be nearby. She felt his presence. They were connected through some unexplainable force.

Mary reached the altar and dismounted. She walked over and sat down on a grassy spot lost in thought. How did events get to the point of Barnamus being killed? In her dreams they were happy here, she felt the love from Barnamus, and the gentleness from Luke. What happened to change that?

Mary began to get drowsy sitting in the sun. She leaned back and was soon asleep.

Her dream took her back to another time here on the Island. Luke was waiting for Barnamus. He couldn't imagine what was keeping him. He was seldom late. Luke went in search of his friend.

Luke heard angry voices. He stopped in fear. Who could these people be. Luke crept closer. He approached the altar with care. This was where all the commotion was taking place.

When he got to where he could see, Luke stopped in horror. Barnamus was on a horse with a noose around his neck. Luke tried to call out but nothing came out of his mouth. Luke knew if he were detected his fate would be as his friends.

Mary awoke with a start. Oh God, how horrible. No wonder Luke didn't talk or trust anyone. He had seen his friend horribly murdered.

Now Mary understood what possessed Luke to live in such isolation. Mary would find him and prove to him all people were not like those people from the past.

Mary stood up and looked around. How long was she asleep? She needed to get back before Pris and Henry worried about her. After all, Mathew was the only one who knew she was out riding.

Mary got back to the stables just in time to run into Henry. He was pacing up and down in front of the stall. As soon as he saw her he went running to her asking, "Where have you been?"

"I was out riding looking for Luke. I dreamed that Luke, Barnamus, and I were walking along the cliffs. I was Maria and was engaged to Barnamus. Luke was our friend."

"Mary, do you hear yourself talking as if you were Maria? You've got to snap out of it. You're not Maria. This island is playing havoc with your mind and emotions."

Mary was offended, she thought Henry would understand. What gave him the right to lecture her. She was her own person. She stomped off in indignation. How dare he, well I'll show him. I know Luke is my friend and I'll prove it. Everyone thinks I'm going mad just like the other Windsor women, but I'm not.

Mary slammed the door when she entered and Pris looked up from her knitting. "Mary, what in the world is the matter dear? I've never seen you like this."

"Henry has the nerve to lecture me, who does he think he is?"

"Calm down Mary, you're so distraught."

"That man thinks I'm loosing my mind, well I'm not and the sooner he leaves the better."

"Mary you don't mean that, do you dear?"

"Yes, Pris, I do mean that. If he can't trust my judgment he's no friend of mine."

Pris was shocked at Mary's behavior, what was happening with her well mannered niece. She would have a talk with Henry and find out what happened. Mary went to her room, shut the door and lay across her bed. She would insist Henry leave. She felt he was responsible for Luke leaving.

Henry returned to the house and looked for Pris. Pris could tell he was in agony. "Henry what happened? Mary was very upset when she came in. I've never seen her so angry."

"Mary returned from her ride and was talking out of her head. Something about Barnamus, Maria, and Luke. The creature we've kept at the cabin, according to Mary, is Luke. Mary believes she's Maria. I tried to get her back to reality, but she stormed off. Pris, I'm more worried about her now than before."

Mary remembered what her mother told her about being the girl in the dream. The girl Barnamus loved, her name was Maria. How could she get her family to believe her? She knew in her heart she was Maria. Luke knew it too, but he was gone. So how could she prove it without Luke?

Mary changed clothes and went down for lunch. One thing for sure she didn't want to see Henry. She slipped in the kitchen and asked Sara if she could have a light lunch to carry with her to the garden.

Sara told her she would fix her a roast beef sandwich, put a piece of fruit and some cold lemonade in the basket for her. "Would you want something fixed for Henry?"

"No, Sara, thank you, I'm not seeing him today, if I can help it."

"What's wrong Mary?"

"Henry thinks I've lost my mind. He doesn't understand Luke the way I do. I tried telling Henry that I was Maria, Barnamus' fiancé, but he thinks I'm mad. Sara, you don't think this do you? My mother even told me I was Maria."

"Mary, I know you believe what your saying, but we don't want to think of that possibility. It's frightening to think of a person having a past life. That you fell to your death and returned as Mary.

"I know a lot of things have taken place here since you arrived, but you need to be patient with us dear. We love you and we only have your best interest at heart.

"Don't judge Henry to harshly. He loves you, why else would he still be here?

"Do you want anyone knowing where you are? Or do you need this time alone?"

"If you would, Sara, let me have this time to think, to try to sort out my feelings. Tell Pris I will see her at dinner and not to worry, I'm fine. I will go to the garden, have my lunch and think about what you've said. You give some pretty good advice Sara, thank you."

Mary went out the side door on her way to the garden, she knew no one would see her leaving the house from this side. The sun was high in the sky and she felt better than she had that morning. Surprising what a little chat with a friend will do for you. And she did consider Sara a good friend.

Mary remembered what her mother told her about being the girl in the dream. The girl Barnamus loved, who was Maria. How could she get her family to believe her. She knew in her heart she was Maria. So how could she prove it without Luke.

Mary walked the path, which was very familiar to her now to the garden. A breeze was gently blowing, the sun was shining, and it was just a beautiful day all around. Maybe she could put the events of this island out of her mind long enough to enjoy this day.

Mary was at the garden now and it was beautiful with all the flowers in bloom. She had put a lot of work in the garden to restore it to its previous state. Mary spread her lunch on the bench and sat down to eat. She hadn't realized she was so hungry. Sara was a terrific cook, and it showed in every meal she prepared.

Mary enjoyed her lunch and after sat back and closed her eyes. You could smell the roses, they were hypnotizing. Mary dozed off to sleep. In her dream she could see Luke coming toward her. She was sitting in the garden alone.

What was wrong with Luke, he looked as if he'd seen a ghost. Luke got to Mary and screamed, "you're dead, you're dead."

Mary was startled when she woke. She quickly looked around, but no one was in the little garden but her.

How could she end these nightmares? What was it she was supposed to know, but was clueless about?

Even though she had eaten she still had some left. No need sitting here all evening, she might as well get up and go see if Luke had decided to return.

Mary would give the remainder of her lunch to Mathew. Mathew was checking the horses' shoes when she saw him. He was singing as he worked. It was such a pretty tune. But she didn't recognize it.

Mathew looked up from his work and smiled at Mary. "Good to see you out and about. I'm sorry if I got you upset. That was not my intentions at all. You do know I care for you deeply. If there's anyway I can help you, please feel free to ask."

Mary picked up on this and told Mathew he could help her. He could help her find Luke and not say a word to Pris or Henry about it. Mathew promised he would do his best and he wouldn't tell a soul.

They discussed several ways of tracking Luke, but still with caution. Even Mary admitted Luke could be dangerous, his concept of reality was unknown.

Maybe he thought she was Maria come back from the dead to haunt this place. The place she died.

Mary only knew she needed to find him. A lot of the secrets she felt lay within Luke. The only person that was still alive, that knew the truth.

Mathew and Mary planned to meet the next day right after sunrise. They would get an early start and cover as much ground as possible.

Luke was not far away and could hear the plans being made to find him. Luke really wanted to let Maria know he was fine, but he was scared. Had Maria come back to life, he saw her hit the water. Maria was dead. Luke was confused. He needed somebody to explain this to him, but Barnamus was dead too.

Luke would visit Maria, maybe he could trust her. She seemed kind, she'd never mistreated him before. Luke was getting time mixed up. What was memories and what was reality? Luke quietly moved away from Mary and Mathew.

Luke needed to rest, he'd not slept much since Sara released him. Luke was afraid of being caught again. He was much more cautious now than before. Luke went back to the hidden cave down the side of the cliff. This was why he'd been so hard to find all these years. Nobody knew of the cave except Luke.

Mary left Mathew and went back to the house. She didn't think she could ever call this home. It just didn't have that special feeling that makes you feel at home. No there was nothing here but sinister feelings that left her cold inside.

Mary went in search of Pris when she got to the house. She felt horrible about worrying her so much lately. She promised herself to be more aware of what she was putting Pris through.

Pris was glad to see her niece. She was safe. When you let your mind wonder you can come up with some pretty horrible stuff. But Pris knew not all the feelings were unfounded. After all she had lived here when Beth was alive and remembered everything that happened to well.

"Mary, I've been so worried. Henry told me you were not yourself and then I couldn't find you. Where have you been?"

"Pris, I'm sorry, I didn't mean to worry you. I got angry with Mathew and Henry. They were treating me as if I were mad. I dreamed about this island during the time Barnamus was alive. In my dream I was Maria. Barnamus brought me here from Brunswick, Georgia. I lived on St. Simons Island just off the Brunswick coast.

"I was to marry him. Luke was a friend of Barnamus. Barnamus cared for Luke and kept him a secret from everyone. Maria loved Luke as soon as she met him. Luke had been abandoned by the midwife, who left him to die on the cliffs because he looked so horrid.

"Barnamus found him and through the years came to care for him. He was Barnamus brother but didn't know this. Neither did Barnamus. Maria was out walking along the cliffs with both of them, when she slipped and fell to her death.

"Both were devastated and Barnamus became recluse and a person started awful lies about him. That's how Barnamus came to be so brutally murdered. The towns people started rumors of missing girls after Maria died. And this one dark stormy night one of the local girls ran off with her beau. The townspeople were drinking and stories started flying around. They got in their boats and came over, took Barnamus captured and hung him. Luke saw the whole thing, was terrified and ran away.

"After that he was afraid of people, and was never seen by anyone again."

"Mary, that's the saddest story I've ever heard. I know you're distraught about Luke, but we're still worried about you. Henry's experience with these type tragedies is not like our family has experienced. It's been this way for us as long as I can remember. First with my mother, then with Beth, and now with us."

"We will make Henry understand we're not crazy women. There evil afoot here and we've got to deal with it." Pris went to talk to Henry, she knew now that Mary was not insane. Everything finally fit into place.

Henry was out walking through the flower garden at the back of the house. Pris approached him, he looked so worried.

"Henry, I've just spoken to Mary. She's fine dear, she is not the raving maniac you thought she was. What she knows is real. Somehow she has seen back in time to the past. Maybe she was Maria. We don't know but she told me the whole story.

"Don't pull away from her she needs us now. It's frightening for her to see and hear these things from a past she feels a part of. She's very worried about Luke."

"Pris, I will be here for her. I hope she doesn't hate me for thinking she was mad. Just help me to understand what I need to do."

"Just love her Henry, hold her hand, and listen without judging."

"I will do my best. I will go to her now and ask forgiveness. Do you know where she is?"

"She's gone to her room to lie down for awhile before dinner. She is exhausted."

"I will see her at dinner then." Pris left Henry in the garden and went in search of Sara.

Sara was in the kitchen putting the last part of the meal together. Sara came across some fresh crab and made crab cakes. In addition she made hush puppies, coleslaw, baked beans, boiled shrimp and deep fried catfish. This was a feast.

Since arriving on the island, they had pretty much stuck with light meals. Sometimes it was just too hot to eat. Mary especially loved seafood. For dessert Sara fixed a blackberry cobbler. Pris realized she was famished.

Mary, Henry, and Mathew came in together for the meal. Pris assumed Henry had spoken to Mary. They were talking at least.

They sat down for their meal and carried on a pleasant conversation. Nothing was mentioned about the morning activities. By the end of dinner everyone was stuffed. There was plenty left over. Mary wished she knew where Luke was. She could take him some food. No use dwelling on that right now.

They adjourned to the parlor for coffee and dessert. Sara brought it in on a tray and put it on the coffee table. She excused herself, saying she wanted to clean the kitchen before it got much later. Everyone offered to help but she refused, telling them to enjoy the coffee and dessert.

Mary watched her curiously. Sara's eyes kept avoiding her own. After Sara left Mary excused herself. Now might be the time to check up on Sara.

Mary watched Sara leave through the side door. Mary was not far behind. Sara seemed to be carrying a basket. Where was she going, and why? Mary followed Sara down the path to the garden. Sara left the basket on the bench looked around and started back up the path. Mary stepped into the woods, so she could not be seen.

CHAPTER SIXTEEN

Mary would wait and see what happened with the basket. Could she be feeding Luke? How would he know to come? Sara knew more than she let on about Luke. Mary would get to the bottom of this. She would settle down and wait.

Luke appeared out of nowhere. Opened the basket and began to eat. Mary slipped quietly out of her hiding place and spoke softly to Luke.

"Luke, it's all right, it's me Mary. I won't hurt you. I've been so worried about you. You think I'm Maria, I understand now. I look like her Luke, but Maria's dead.

"I know what you've lived through, the horror of Barnamus death. Luke trust me, I'm sorry about the chains. No wonder you were so frightened. Please just let me be your friend. I won't tell the others I've found you."

Luke had not moved. He wanted to be near Mary. As long as they left him free he could trust himself not to harm her.

Mary was happy Luke was still there and had not run away. She wouldn't get too close for now, he needed to be able to trust her. "Luke I must return to the house before they miss me. I will meet you tomorrow evening here in the garden. I hope you understand what I'm saying.

Mary told Luke goodnight and turned and slipped back up the path the way she came earlier. Mary entered through the side door, Sara had neglected to lock it. She went down the hall and entered the parlor.

Pris noticed as she entered. "Mary, we thought you might have gone to bed."

"No, I was just doing some preparations for tomorrow. I needed to wash out a few things so they would dry over night." Mary asked if Sara was finished in the kitchen."

"I haven't seen her since she left before you did."

"Pris, I will check on her and see if she needs help."

Mary walked to the kitchen and found Sara finishing the dishes. "Sara do you need any help? We were all worried about you. Why don't you come join us for coffee and cobbler?"

"Thanks, Mary, but I think I'll turn in early. It's been a long day."

Mary told Sara she would see her in the morning and left the kitchen. It had been a long tiring day, she went back to the parlor and bid everyone goodnight.

Even though Mary had changed rooms, this one was as cold as the other one. She might as well face it. She was being haunted.

Mary drifted off to sleep, at least she knew where Luke was now and she was determined to win his trust. She slept pretty good for the first time in weeks.

Mary woke up refreshed eager to start a new day. She would meet Luke at the garden later, but for now she was expected to meet Mathew. She would go through the motion of looking for a few days with Mathew then just pretend it was no use hunting him.

Mathew was waiting for Mary. He thought of some places Luke might be hiding. They'd check them today. Mathew really hoped they didn't succeed in there adventure. This creature had been here a long time, why try and change him now. It made no sense to Mathew. But he promised to help, so help he would.

Instead of riding Mathew and Mary walked. That would make looking easier. Mary enjoyed walking on the island anyway. The different sounds from the wildlife you heard as you walked. The fleeting glance of a deer watering, or wild hogs feeding. The cry of seagulls. All of this would lead you to believe this was paradise. But that was far from the truth. They had been walking for about an hour, when Mathew needed to stop and take a break. It was a very humid day. Some places they'd covered you couldn't get the benefit of the ocean breeze.

The foliage was dense. The palmetto bushes were everywhere, so you had to be careful not to get stuck by the sharp ends. Palm trees were plentiful but didn't allow for much shade.

More inland was oaks, dogwoods, and pines, deeper in there were areas of cypress trees. The Spanish moss swayed in the breeze. The limbs were covered in moss. In the dusk of evening it was an eerie sight to behold.

The dense areas were populated with mosquitoes, deerflies, and gnats. Between the deerfly and gnat it was unbearable. The deerfly had a terrible bite which whelped up and itched. The sand gnat burned when it defecated on you and you'd get blotches that looked like the measles. These bites itched for days.

All in all it was miserable going in these areas. Mary was more than happy to stop for Mathew and put ointment on her bites. She voted for them to go back to the beach area where the breeze would keep these pest away from them.

She pitied her horses and was glad Mathew rubbed them down every morning before daylight with special oils to protect them from these horrible bugs. How did Luke survive this and the elements of nature all these years?

Along this coastal area was well known for hurricanes and tropical storms. Where did Luke escape from the torrent rains and wind? He must have a place nobody ever found. But where?

Mary suggested they head back, it was getting midday the hottest part of the day. “We will try again tomorrow. But we will take the horses instead of walking in this heat.” Mathew was glad to hear this. The heat was getting worse everyday for him. He would like to live somewhere up North where it stayed cool year round.

They got back to the stables and Mary left Mathew to go to the house. Not far from the stables she ran into Luke. He came out into the path in front of her.

“Luke, I’m so glad to see you. Mathew and I were out for a walk today. He thinks we’re looking for you, but we’re not. I will meet you at the garden before the sun goes down. I hope you understand me.”

Luke nodded. Mary felt a glimmer of hope that he did understand. “Until tonight my friend.”

Mary walked on toward the house. Luke must be following me, how else would he know where I was. This was good, he wanted to be near her. This gave her hope of helping him to adjust to being with someone for the first time in many, many years.

Mary was hungry, she sailed in the backdoor and was greeted by Sara. “Sara, I’m starved, got anything for a growing girl?” Sara laughed and told her to help herself to a dish of chicken salad and some fruit. This sounded good to Mary.

Mary wanted to ask Sara about last night. Well might as well plunge in. “Sara forgive me for snooping, but I followed you last night to the garden.” Sara looked pale. “Sara it’s alright I’m glad your feeding Luke. I just want to know how you’re connected to him.”

Sara told Mary to have a seat and eat while she filled her in on the story. Sara told Mary the story of how she came about looking after Luke. “I’m glad he was cared for by you Sara. So the stories from my dreams are real. Everything you told me I already knew except about you caring for him. Sara I talked to him last night after you left. I think he understands me. I will take his food tonight. I've made plans to meet him before sundown. I saw him on the way here. I think he's following me. He thinks I'm Maria.

"I want to help him, Sara, not harm him. I will never allow anyone to hurt him again. I want his trust and friendship."

So at this point Mary started caring for Luke. She would spend hours with him. On one such occasion she made him laugh out loud. He looked shocked that he could still make such sounds. Mary was thrilled.

Mathew, Henry and Pris had no idea she was spending time with Luke. They'd meet in different places everyday. Mary began teaching Luke the language he stopped using a long time ago.

Luke's trust grew daily toward Mary. He enjoyed their time together and longed for more. He knew he was still a secret to the rest of the people except Sara.

The weeks passed. Luke and Mary drew closer and closer. Luke totally trusted her and finally realized she was not Maria but Mary.

Mary found in the past few weeks nobody questioned her anymore about her activities of the day. She didn't know if maybe it was because they knew she was with Luke or the fact she was looking better these days.

All Mary knew was that she was happy and she was even able to forgive Henry and continue their relationship.

Now Mary faced her biggest challenge, getting Luke to come back to the cottage and stay. There would be no chains, or any type restraints this time. He would be free to come and go as he pleased. Mary mentioned this to Luke on one of these meetings. Luke looked scared for a moment, then told her he would do this for her. Mary told Luke she would let everyone know what they'd been up too for the last several weeks and that Luke was coming back of his own free will.

Mary promised Luke she would let nothing hurt him and she would be there everyday with him. "There still so much I can teach you. First, I'd like to cut your hair and buy you some clothes. These animal hides you wear would be replaced with clothes like Henry and Mathew wear. I know it will take some getting used to, but I know you can.

"Then there the deal with sleeping. We sleep in beds. They're warm and comfortable. I know you don't understand what that means because of the way you've lived all your life. But you will see what I mean."

Mary would send Henry to the mainland for the clothes that would fit him next time the boat came over. The people at the shop would think they were for Henry. Mary was very tired and wanted to go to bed to get some rest.

Mary fell asleep and dreamed peaceful dreams. She awoke early and crawled out of bed. It looked like it would be a beautiful day. It was nice to be up before everyone, it gave her time to think. She dressed and went downstairs. She needed some coffee. Mary would go ahead and start breakfast. It was too early to wake Sara.

By the time the coffee was finished Henry joined her. "You're up with the birds this morning! What's so important that you got up at this time of morning?"

"Oh, nothing. I like to see the sunrise sometimes."

"A girl after my own heart."

"Would you like some coffee and something to eat?"

"Coffee would be nice but it's too early to eat." They drank their coffee on the veranda and waited for everyone else to awaken before eating their meal. For Mary it was nice being alone with Henry for a while this morning.

Henry asked Mary if she would like to ride for a while after they ate. Mary told him that she would but after she would need to check on their friend. "I think he is coming along fine, but I'm getting jealous of the time you spend with him instead of with me."

"It's all for a good cause. I need to find out things from him I can't find out any other way."

"I really understand, it's important to you. Let's have breakfast and saddle the horses for that ride."

Mathew wasn't at the stable, so Henry saddled the horses and away they went. It was around ten o'clock in the morning when they got back. Mary left Henry at the stable and went to the cabin. The haircut helped his appearance quite a bit, so she knew clothes would do even more for him.

His appearance wasn't as ghastly now as it was a few hours ago. Now, if she could just get a tub of water here and get him bathed. Mary knew that would certainly be a major undertaking. But Mary was determined to give him a bath. She would have Henry and Mathew attempt this. Mary just wished she knew who would win Henry and Mathew, or her friend.

Henry came to the cabin and couldn't believe the change only a haircut made. Maybe there was hope, after all. Mary told Henry about the bath she planned for her friend. Henry didn't know too much about that, but he agreed to give it a try, the things he would do for Mary. He must be in love. He went in search of Mathew for help to give Luke a bath. Henry knew they were in for trouble. They got the tub from the house and filled it with water they heated on the fire. Henry grabbed plenty of soap and towels. It would probably take more than one bath to clean him up, but he would take all day if necessary. Henry and Mathew went into the cabin and told their friend that Mary wanted them to bathe him. When he saw the water he went wild. Henry knew Mary would have to be there during this ordeal to keep him calm.

He still didn't trust Henry or Mathew, so there was a wrestling match between the three. Mary couldn't remember ever seeing anything quite as funny in her whole life. She didn't know who was really getting a bath, Henry, Mathew or her friend. After the first scrubbing the creature didn't mind the water as much. He really looked better after he was clean. In just one day they changed his appearance completely. Now Mary would find him a bed and teach him to sleep in it, like a normal person.

All three went to the main house to eat lunch. After all that tussling with Mary's friend they were pretty tired. During lunch they told Pris and Sara about the bath. And how much effort it took to accomplish this task.

Sara couldn't believe what she was hearing. She would go later and see for herself. Mary told Pris she was going to take one of the beds from upstairs down to the cabin for him to sleep on. Pris asked Henry what were they going to do with Mary. "Next thing you know she'll have him moving in to the house."

"Pris, I have a long way to go before I can do that."

"Lord, child you mean you actually considered the idea?"

"Yes, it's crossed my mind."

"Henry, what are we going to do with her?" It was good to see Mary smile again, she seemed to be very happy lately working with

Luke trying to help him. The name really fit, he just seemed like a Luke.

Mary and Henry went upstairs and started to take down one of the beds. "This will do for a while, Henry."

They moved it down to the cabin and set it up. Mary showed Luke how to sleep on it and he seemed to understand. "Now you will no longer live like an animal." Henry could see the caring in Mary's eyes as she talked to Luke. On the way home he would ask her to marry him. They started up the path when Henry stopped.

"Don't worry Mary, I'll not let you go. I love you very much. Will you do me the honor of being my wife?"

"Yes, Henry that would make me the happiest person alive. Let's go tell Pris and Mathew and Sara. Oh, Henry our lives will be perfect. I love you so very much."

CHAPTER SEVENTEEN

They entered the house and found Pris. She was thrilled with the news. Finally she wouldn't have to worry about Mary. She wanted to sit down and discuss the arrangements with Mary. It would be a fine wedding.

Henry went off and left the women to talk, he was going to find Mathew and ask him to be his best man. He wanted to take Mary to meet his family. They would love her as much as he did. Mathew was very pleased and surprised about the announcement. He knew Henry was good for Mary. Mathew and Henry went back to the house to talk to Pris and Mary. They needed to discuss the plans for the up coming wedding. Mathew felt a longing in his heart for Pris. She was a very fine lady he knew that the day he met her.

Maybe if things went right this would be a double wedding. He would talk to Pris later and let her know how he felt.

Mary and Pris were busy talking over plans about the wedding, where it would be held, who would be invited, what would be served and things like that. A man would have no idea what they were really talking about. Mary wanted a simple wedding with Henry's parents attending. She couldn't make up her mind where she wanted to go for the honeymoon.

While Mary was talking to Pris, she remembered Luke. "Oh Pris, how will I tell Luke where he will understand? He doesn't understand much and I'm beginning to make some progress with him. He's beginning to trust me. What if this makes him withdraw again? I have to find Henry and tell him of this predicament." Mary went to find Henry to discuss this with him. She didn't want to hurt Luke and she knew by getting married she might be doing a lot of damage. Maybe Henry could come up with a solution. Mary found Henry at the stables; he knew something was wrong when he saw her.

Mary explained her problem to him and asked what she should do. Henry told Mary to let him think about it for a while. He couldn't wait to make her his wife. He wanted to tell her of the plans he thought of. He wanted to take her to Savannah to meet his parents and then the four of them make a return trip to the island. That way Mary could shop for her dress.

Mary thought that was wonderful except she would have to leave Luke. She would entrust his care to Pris. Mary went back to the house to fix dinner for her friend. On the way home she thought of all the things that happened since arriving. Things changed so much since Henry came to visit and stayed to make sure she was safe.

Mary slept better lately and she began to look more like her old self. The dreams stopped since seeing her mother, but at times she could feel something pulling at her. She didn't want to think about it now for she was much too happy. She couldn't wait to become Mrs. Henry Collins. They would be happy here on her island, she just knew they would. Mary fixed Luke dinner and took it back to him.

Luke was very hungry when Mary got his food to him. Mary sat with him while he ate. She mentioned leaving for a while to see how he would react. He jumped up suddenly and began to roam the room. "Luke, it's alright. I'm coming back. I just want to go away for a few days to shop in Savannah. You can't get what you need unless you go yourself to be fitted for clothes.

"Pris will take care of you while I'm gone or I wouldn't leave you.

"You've got to learn to trust me. I will not lie to you I want to be your friend. And friends don't lie to one another. Do you understand?"

For the first time Luke spoke.

Luke took her hand and said, "I understand, Mary." She hoped he understood. She couldn't really tell what he did understand. Luke finished his supper and Mary returned to the house.

Mathew, Henry and Pris were waiting for her. She spent more time with Luke tonight. Mary explained what she told Luke and how it upset him. "Maybe by the time I leave he will be used to the idea. Pris, you need to go with me everyday so he will get used to you. Luke's so frightened of everyone, I feel so sorry for him."

After dinner they sat for a while in the parlor and Henry told them a little about his childhood. He was born in Savannah, Georgia. At the age of six he was sent to a fine old southern school for boys. He made it home for holidays and vacations. He rarely saw his parents, they were very active socially. The servants took care of him when he was home. But all in all he was a happy child he loved riding and there were plenty of places for a young boy to play.

Henry told them of the children he hoped to have and the time he would devote to them. He didn't want to ship them off to boarding schools, he would have tutors to come to them. Of course, they would have help for the house and grounds.

It was around eleven when everyone retired for the night. Mary sat at the window looking out for a while before undressing for bed. She couldn't believe she was so happy. Sometime in the wee hours of the morning she fell asleep. She awoke with a chill. Her room was cold again so she got up for a blanket. She passed the mirror and from the reflection of the moon she saw herself in the mirror. The woman that looked back at her was dressed completely in black. She screamed and fainted, dead to the world.

Henry heard her and went running into her room. Mary lay passed out on the floor. Henry lifted her in his arms and carried her to her bed. Pris wasn't long behind Henry and went to get a cold cloth for Mary. When they brought Mary too she looked around half scared to death.

"Mary, what did you see?"

"I passed the mirror and looked around. I was dressed completely in black."

"Mary, you probably imagined that since it wasn't very light in here."

"Henry, you believe me don't you? I know what I saw, it was me dressed in mourning clothes. I was just beginning to shake all the old feelings I've felt since I came here. Now I'm scared again it all comes flooding back."

"Mary, I will stay here with you till morning. Maybe you can sleep some before dawn."

"Just don't leave me Henry."

Pris went back to bed and Henry sat on the side of Mary's bed holding her hand. She mumbled in her sleep and tossed and turned. It was as if something was chasing her. Henry wanted to get her out of here as soon as possible for her own well being.

Mary woke and seemed to be more in control. Henry told her to stay in bed but she refused. "I have to start getting Pris ready to take over Luke's care. I want this trip now more than ever. I need to get away for a while and see if things will get back to normal. Are you sure you want to marry me with all my problems?"

"I love you, Mary and that's all that matters. Lets go down for breakfast. I'll go dress and wait for you in the hall. I love you very much and always will."

Mary didn't want to look in the mirror so she combed her hair and left it down. She met Henry in the hall about fifteen minutes later and they joined Pris and Mathew in the dinning room. Pris asked Mary how she felt.

"Kind of rattled, that woman scared me to death. I wish I knew what it all means but I'm afraid to find out.

"Pris are you ready to meet Luke this morning? I want to get him used to you so I can leave. I need this trip more than ever."

Pris could see that Mary really did at this point. They took a tray and went to see Luke. He was very nervous around Pris but after a while he calmed down with her.

Mary knew that Pris would have no trouble with Luke. Today Mary was going to take Luke to the stream. She took him out before and it was fine. Luke was learning quickly what pleased Mary. It wouldn't be long before he could move into the house. Luke exhibited very good manners now and was very protective of Mary. He still hadn't taken to Henry, but Mary hoped they would be friends. "Luke, I saw myself last night in the mirror dressed in black it frightened me. I was in my night gown and it was white. I looked as if I were lost. I felt a chill as I looked at myself, as if my whole world just disappeared."

"Mary, I won't let anything or anyone hurt you. You care about me like no one else and I will take care of you." She wanted to find a way to tell him about Henry. It must be the right time. They enjoyed the day together and returned to the cabin. Luke was working on a secret surprise for Mary.

The weeks passed and Pris took to Luke, they formed a special bond. Luke was almost as glad to see Pris as he was Mary. These were two special women and he loved them both. Mary thought it was time to move him to the house. He was excited about living with these women not being far away from either of them. He roamed around the house marveling at all its beauty.

CHAPTER EIGHTEEN

Several weeks passed and Mary was ready for her trip. Luke accepted she was leaving but would be back. She promised to write to him and tell him all about Savannah. On the day she and Henry left Luke walked them to the docks. "Mary, I'm looking forward to your return. I'll miss you terribly."

"And I'll miss you Luke, take care of Pris for me while I'm away."

"You know I will let nothing hurt her, I promise."

Henry and Mary were on their way. They were to catch a boat in Pineda. They would be at sea for six days before they hit the Georgia coast. His parents would meet them at the Savannah docks. Henry and Mary had adjoining cabins. Henry knew how the crew would treat an unescorted woman. He stayed close to her at all times.

Mary was a beautiful woman. He was proud of her and proud to be in her company. He would treasure her all his life. They were blessed with smooth sailing all the way and the trip did wonders for Mary. She looked very healthy, the sea air seemed to agree with her.

Brian and Helen Collins met them at the docks and took them to Camilla Plantation just outside of Savannah. Mary loved the scenery. Everything was in bloom and the ride was wonderful. The plantation was on the shore. From her window Mary could see the breakers. There were about twenty servants in the house, the house was very spacious with thirty rooms. Mr. Collins said they owned about two thousand slaves that worked his cotton fields. They raised everything they needed to eat as well as the cotton.

Henry's dad prided himself on his thoroughbred horses. Henry showed Mary all of his secret places around the plantation which made Mary feel closer than ever to him.

That night at dinner she told Brian and Helen a little about herself and how she met Henry. They both liked her immediately she was like the daughter they never had. They felt a sadness from her but they wouldn't pry they would let her come to them when she was ready. They felt Henry already knew of her trouble. He asked for a room next to his for her and he rarely left her side. The Collins's were really enjoying the children being there. Mary ate things that night that she previously knew nothing of and enjoyed them immensely.

By bed time, she was exhausted and ready for a good nights sleep. She dreamed wonderful dreams that night of running through these magnificent woods with Henry. The next morning, she was refreshed and looked radiant. Helen thought she was beautiful and could be of royal decent. Henry laughed and told her she was correct that Mary was a countess. Helen was amazed, "So you have royal blood, child. Now I know who you are. You're of the Windsor family of Florida."

"Yes, my father was Sir Windsor of Windsor Palace. When he married my mother he moved to Singer Island just across from Pineda, Florida."

"You knew neither your mother or father?"

"No, after my mother died my aunt raised me. My father left me the island on my eighteenth birthday.

"I can understand the pain he went through he loved my mother very much. Living with me would have been too much on him.

"I would have loved to have known him but it's too late now. Henry and I want a big family to fill up our home. I've always loved children and I think we would make good parents. We both have a lot of love to offer."

"Yes, Henry was alone a lot when he was growing up. We regret we didn't take more time to be with him. We won't make that mistake with our grandchildren. You can come stay as long as you like with us."

"Helen, we would love it."

"I know you will love the island it's so quite and peaceful. You're in a world all your own. Sometimes I wonder if anything exists but us. The people from the mainland are afraid of Singer Island they won't come near it."

"Why are they afraid?"

"Mother, please let us not speak about it there have been some things that have happened to Mary since moving to the island."

"Alright, dear, we won't speak of it again, unless Mary wants to talk to us. Let's talk about your wedding gown. You'll need a new wardrobe. While you're here we can get everything that's needed. We have a lot to do in a short time. We want to show you off to our friends. We're happy to have you dear.

"Now we need to change and meet my dressmaker at eleven. She does excellent work and with your figure she'll have no problems with you, your complexion goes with everything."

After the fitting they went shopping and Mary bought gifts for Luke, Pris, Mathew, and Sara. She found a beautiful ring she bought for Henry. It was a lion made of gold with rubies for eyes and a diamond in its mouth. Mary bought a beautiful fan for Helen and a pipe for Brian. After lunch she and Helen returned to the house.

Henry met the coach when it pulled up to the house and helped the ladies out as he lifted Mary down he swirled her around and around. "I missed you, Mary. Please don't get too far away from me again."

"I promise, Henry I won't. I missed you, too. I bought you something. I thought you would like it caught my eye and I just had to get it for you." Henry was overjoyed with Mary's present it was remarkable, he had seldom seen anything like it. He put it on with pride, it would not leave his hand. Mary and Henry enjoyed the evening riding around looking at the plantation.

Mary asked about the slaves and why they had them. "Mary, they're not educated enough to care for themselves, so we take care of them in exchange for the work they do in our fields. We don't believe in mistreating them. Neither Father nor I would stand for that. There have been some bad ones come through. We'd have to watch them closely until we could get them moved, but even those we did not mistreat. I enjoy hearing the people singing around the fire at night after work. I'll bring you down to the quarters one night and let you meet some of our people." Henry pulled the wagon up to a stream and both got out. Henry put his arm around Mary and told her she was the most enchanting person he'd ever seen. "I feel like the luckiest man on earth to have you my darling. Please don't allow anything or anybody to come between us."

"I would not do that, Henry. I love you with my heart and soul. When the last breath is leaving my body my love will stay with you through all time. I get scared, Henry."

"I love you my darling."

"When I saw myself in that black dress I wasn't afraid for myself, but for you. Please be careful in anything you do."

"Nothing will happen, Mary. I won't let it."

"Sometimes fate can be cheated and, if possible, we will cheat fate."

They rode back to the house and Mary went up for a bath and to get ready for dinner. Lois laid Mary's garments out for her and her bath drawn.

Lois helped Mary undress and get into the tub. Lois washed her hair and when she was finished it gleamed. Mary learned that Lois was born at Camilla Plantation and was very happy here. "Master, he be good to us slaves. We has decent clothes, plenty food and gets to go to church on Sunday, like white folk."

"Lois, have you ever thought about leaving Camilla?"

"No ma'am I's be happy here."

"I know you'd be happy on Singer Island, Lois. It's beautiful."

"I's wouldn' like the thought of living on an island. I's scared of water ma'am."

Mary laughed and told Lois it would be alright there was a huge Island where she wouldn't have to see the ocean unless she wanted to. "Please, hand me the towel, before I shrivel up."

Lois helped Mary dress and fixed her long dark hair on top of her head. "Thank you, Lois, you're so good with my hair."

"You's show is purty misses. Now I's knows why Master Henry be took with you so. You's a fine gentle woman, you is."

"You're very kind, Lois. If you ever change your mind I would love to take you home with me."

"Thank you, ma'am, I's don't get much of a choice what's I wants ma'am and I wants to thank you from the bottom of this old black heart."

Mary joined Henry and Brain in the library. "Aren't you lovely my dear I see what Henry saw in you. These old eyes could never get tired of looking at you."

"What a flirt you are becoming, Brian. I'll have to keep an eye on you with our new daughter-in-law."

"Helen you're still the prettiest belle these old eyes have ever seen."

Mary noticed the look between Brian and Helen and knew they were still very much in love. She hoped it would be the same between her and Henry after twenty or thirty years.

To Henry's delight, Mary was looking much better. He knew if she got away from Singer Island for a while it would do her a world of good. She seemed to love the old plantation from the first. The slaves intrigued her, the kids amused her and she loved the music they played every night around the fires in front of their shanties.

They had been in Savannah now for about four weeks and everything was almost completed. Soon they would be returning to

Singer Island to be married. He didn't mind taking her back there now for she would be his wife. He missed Pris and Mathew very much and even Luke in a strange way.

He wondered how Luke had fared since Mary had been gone. He hoped Luke made progress since there absence. For some strange reason he couldn't understand, she was determined to take care of Luke.

He was lost in thought when his mother brought him back to reality. "Son, what day are we to go to Mary's Island? I have to get everything here in order before we leave with you."

"I think, if Mary's rested and ready by Saturday, we will depart. Will that give you enough time, Mother?"

"Three days is enough, Henry, to make sure the plantation will be looked after. Brain and I have decided to stay on the Island for a few weeks to enjoy the weather. I can't wait to meet Pris, she seems such a charming woman."

Everything was set in motion for them to depart on Saturday. Trunks were packed, decisions regarding what to pack and what to leave were made. It was a mad house for a couple of days.

Henry and Brain decided to stay clear for a while so they took a ride around the estate. Brian told Henry he was very proud of his choice for his wife. "She is from a very good blood line and will bear many a fine grandchild." Neither knew the past of the women of Singer Island. Henry knew some but not all.

For almost a month now the dreams hadn't plagued her sleep at night but the closer she came to returning to the Island the more she wondered if those dreams would return.

She saw her mother, she knew Henry had seen her also. Mary knew what she had seen was not just in her mind. She knew her mother would protect her as much as was possible from whatever pulled at her from the past. Mary just wanted to lead a normal life with Henry and their children. She couldn't let Henry know the fear she still felt of unknown things from her past. She just prayed everything would work out for the best.

On Friday, everything was ready for their journey back to the Island. The boat was loaded in readiness for the journey. Now it only awaited its passengers to set sail. On their last night in Georgia, their evening at the plantation was pleasant.

Mary would miss the dancing and music of the slaves at night. She would even miss her maid for the friendship they had built between them.

At the same time it would be nice to get home to Pris and Luke. She had not been away from Pris this long in all her eighteen years. She hoped that by now Mathew had made a move toward letting Pris know how he cared for her. She knew they loved each other but were too set in their ways to make much of the matter. She thought about her friend Luke, who trusted her. She hadn't told Henry's parents about him yet. She knew that she must before they got to the island. She didn't know how much Pris, Mathew and Sara had accomplished since she left. She hoped he hadn't forgotten her.

"Oh well," she didn't want to think about it for now. Henry wanted to go to the slave quarters to watch the dancing one last time before they left tomorrow. They couldn't be up very late they were to board very early in the morning.

He hoped it would be a nice smooth trip for the ladies. He and Brian were used to rough seas. They both seemed to thrive on it. "I guess it brings out the man from within."

Mary was sad to see their time end so soon. But the slaves rose early to work the fields. They all wished their young master good night and a safe and happy trip. They congratulated him on his forthcoming marriage to Miss Mary.

Mr. and Mrs. Collins were in bed when Henry and Mary returned to the house. Henry poured a brandy for himself and Mary a glass of sherry.

They sat on the porch for a while talking about the trip home. "Henry, this was a wonderful trip. I've met some people whose friendship I will cherish and your parents are wonderful. I can tell they are still very much in love after all these years. I know we will be like that when we're their age. Our home will be over run with grandchildren, it will be so wonderful. I love you, Henry, with all my heart. I'm proud to be the future Mrs. Henry Collins. Together we will make Singer Island flourish with life and activities again. It's a lovely place to raise children."

As soon as they returned the wedding would take place as soon as possible.

No one but the families and a friend or two would attend.

Henry kissed Mary goodnight and they both went to bed. It had been a very long day for everyone. Mary drifted into a peaceful sleep for a few hours only to awaken to a cold room. She looked about and saw herself standing in black in front of the mirror. "Be careful" were the only words spoken and then the apparition disappeared.

Mary went to Henry's door and knocked. Henry arose and went to her. She was as white as a ghost and chilled to the bone. "Mary, what's happened? You look awful."

"Henry, I awoke from a bad dream, that's all."

But he knew there was more to it. Henry didn't push it, he just wrapped her up and carried her and put her in his bed.

"I will sit here beside you while you sleep. Nothing will hurt you I will make sure of that."

Mary felt safe again so she went back to sleep. She felt so bad that Henry slept in a chair all night he looked beat. They were all up at five in the morning, having breakfast and coffee and preparing to leave for the ship.

After breakfast, everyone said farewell and set off for the docks in Savannah. It would be about an hour's ride that would put them on Singer Island around seven in the morning. Everything was already loaded aboard the ship, so they only had to board. Mary looked forward to the journey.

They were under way by eight. She and Helen sat on deck for a while enjoying the sea breeze and sunshine. Around eleven thirty Helen suggested tea and scones with butter and slices of ham for everyone. Mary hadn't realized she was so hungry. She knew it must be the salt air that gave her such an appetite. Henry and Brain joined them in the galley for a light lunch.

They discussed plans over lunch concerning the wedding. Mary told them all that the only people attending would be Pris, Mathew, Sara and Luke. It was to be a small wedding since no one she knew could make the journey on such short notice. A Minister was to come over from the mainland to perform the ceremony. Everything was ready and waiting for their return.

Brain suggested a game of chess to Henry, who accepted. He loved a good, challenging game with his father.

Mary and Helen went strolling around deck. "Helen, there's something I must tell you about Luke. When I first arrived on Singer

Island I ran across this wild creature that scared the life out of me, or I thought it was a creature.

"For months, I would run across him. I could not get near him and to tell the truth I was scared to. When Henry came and found out about him, he and Mathew set a trap for him. We caught him and chained him in a cabin. Everyday I worked with him and got him used to having us around him. It took a lot of work and patience, but I knew he could be like us. He couldn't talk. I cut his hair and sent Henry for some clothes for him. I taught him to eat properly and to read and write. I named him Luke and now he lives with us in the cottage. He's very devoted to me, he seems to be accepting Henry but he's jealous of the time we spend together.

"I guess he has adult emotions, but he acts like a child. I was afraid to leave him, but he seemed to adjust to Pris, so I left with Henry. I have no idea what we will find when we return so I thought I'd better warn you. I only know a little of his past. Since he was an adolescent he roamed the woods alone, living as an animal would. He has appointed himself as my protector. I guess that's only natural since I've spent so much time with him. You don't have to be frightened of him; I don't really think he's dangerous."

"Mary you're a brave and gentle girl to undertake what you have with Luke. How did you manage to get over the fright of him?"

"Helen, I was terrified until I looked into those helpless eyes pleading with me to help him. I was compelled to try to make a man of him. For a long time I couldn't get near him, but as each day passed I would get closer and closer, talking to him, letting him know I wouldn't hurt him. After he accepted me, I could sit with him, cut his hair, shave him, and finally get him to wear clothes. Now, it was quite a job for Henry and Mathew to dress him, I guess to him it was like being chained again. Then, gradually, when I thought he wouldn't run away, we started going outside. We would take walks and I'd tell him what he was seeing like trees, squirrels, birds, deer, ducks and flowers. Things he'd lived with everyday of his life but didn't know what they were called."

"Now I know Henry has found himself a woman in a million. I hope you'll be happy with your life with Henry."

Mary found in her new mother-in-law a real and understanding friend. Brain and Henry were still engrossed in their chess game when Mary went to take a nap. She was so tired from the hustle of the past few days. The voyage was smooth and the gentle rocking of the boat put her to sleep.

She must have slept for two hours when she felt someone in the room with her. She sat up and looked around. It was shadowy in her room and her eyes needed to adjust. Then she saw the woman in black again. The woman looked at her and wept. "Don't return to the Island, Mary. For your sake, go back. Don't journey on." Then she was gone.

Mary sat there in total shock, not understanding any of these things. She must talk to Henry now, she couldn't stand being alone for another moment. She jumped up and ran to Henry's cabin. She knocked furiously. He opened the door to find Mary standing there in her gown. He pulled her into his room and wrapped his robe around her. She was trembling and looked as if she had seen a ghost. Mary told Henry what she saw when she awoke.

They sat and talked for the rest of the night. Henry got a brandy into her. After a while, she calmed down and relaxed against his broad shoulders. He didn't know what was haunting her, but he was going to find out.

She couldn't stand up under such pressure. He sat there wondering if maybe they should stay on the mainland until he could find out what was going on. They were only a few days from Singer Island and he needed to persuade her to stay off the Island for a while. He knew it would be hard but he would find a way.

CHAPTER NINETEEN

Henry woke Mary to get dressed to go to the galley for breakfast. His mom and dad were already there, waiting for them to join them for breakfast. Helen noticed the paleness of Mary's skin as soon as she walked in. She would talk to her to see if there was something she could do. Just to listen might help Mary. The poor child looked a fright. Brain didn't say much but he asked Henry what was wrong with Mary.

"She just didn't sleep too well last night, Dad. She had a bad dream." He knew they wouldn't understand about the insanity that plagued her family.

Henry knew that he alone could work through this with Mary so she wouldn't feel ashamed of her families past. They got through breakfast and went to stroll on deck. He vowed to make the rest of the journey pleasant for Mary. They lay around in the sun the rest of the day, just resting. Mary dozed off a couple of times. Henry was glad, he knew how Mary was sleeping lately. Mary said nothing of the woman in black, but Henry knew she was thinking about her. Months before, he had seen that same woman on the Island and he knew how frightening it could be to see something like that. But what he couldn't understand was since they weren't on the Island how did the woman follow her? Was she really in that much danger?

Now Henry really began to worry. He wouldn't get too far from her, he was afraid to at this point. He would set up a cot in her cabin and watch over her at night. She seemed awful quiet today and Henry tried to cover up for her. But he knew his mother noticed. She fell in love with Mary from the moment she laid eyes on her. Maybe his mother would understand, he just didn't know. He'd think about it for a while, before he said anything to his mother about the lady in black.

Helen watched Henry and Mary very closely; she knew something was wrong but she couldn't put her finger on it. She would just watch and wait for Henry or Mary to trust her.

The day went by slow for all.

Mary was exhausted. She told Henry she was going to take a nap before dinner. Henry said he thought he'd do the same. After they left Helen and Brain, he told Mary he'd sit in a chair in her room while she slept.

Mary was very thankful for him and his presence; she felt safe with him near. She lay down, fell asleep with no trouble and dreamed of being on a lovely beach. She was feeling free and safe, but then everything turned ugly. Off in the distance, down by the shoreline, the woman in black floated toward her. She turned and started to run but the woman gained on her and she couldn't get away.

Henry saw Mary thrashing around on the bed. He wondered what she was dreaming. He decided to wake her up because she was trembling from fright. She told Henry of her dream.

He needed to find out more about the curse of Barnamus Hillards . Henry would go to the town hall and search the records. Surely something was on file there to help explain some of these mysterious happenings. Mary knew it tied in with Barnamus somehow. If she were in danger she would face it head on. Too many people were involved, she would find some answers.

The boat arrived in Pineda the following Saturday. Henry tried to persuade Mary to stay on the mainland but Mary wouldn't hear of it. "I can't run away, Henry. If I do I'll be running all my life. It followed me to Savannah so there's no place to hide from whatever is haunting me."

Mary and Henry arrived on the island around three in the morning. Henry's parents stayed at Pineda for the remainder of the night so that Mary could get everything ready for them. Upon their arrival, the house was dark and forbidding. Mary shivered as she walked to the door. Mary reached for the door and a hideous bony hand grabbed her wrist. Mary screamed and tried to pull away, but the hand held on to her tightly.

Henry saw nothing and was shocked over Mary's behavior. Henry grabbed her and held her until she was exhausted from thrashing around. Mary's screams awakened the house. Sara was the first one to the door. Her eyes were big and round. She didn't have any idea what was happening. They didn't expected Mary and Henry at three in the morning. Pris was next to come through the door. She too was shaken up from the hideous screams that awakened her.

Henry picked Mary up and carried her inside. She kept mumbling, "Did you see it Henry, did you see it?"

Henry had no idea what she was talking about, she was hysterical. It must have been pretty bad for this kind of reaction. Sara got Mary a sherry. The child looked as if she'd seen a ghost. She loved Mary and hated to see her so distraught. Pris kept asking Henry what happened. Henry could only shake his head, "I don't know. Mary reached for the door and went into hysterics."

Mary was drinking her sherry feeling a little better now. What grabbed her at the door, were her eyes playing tricks on her? Was it exhaustion from the trip and all the dreams and the woman in black? Her nerves were on edge from everything.

Pris sat down beside her and took her hand. "Mary, what happened tonight to make you so scared?"

Mary began to tell them what happened. They all looked at her in disbelief. Henry didn't see anything. He was seriously wondering about her sanity at this point. But he'd seen the woman in black upstairs not too many months ago. Maybe all of them were loosing their minds. He knew now he must tell his parents before they came here and experienced something on their own.

Mary refused to sleep, she was afraid to close her eyes so everyone was up for the remainder of the night. Sara made coffee and sweet rolls for everyone.

Pris asked Henry why he brought her back here, but she knew the answer before she asked. Mary was a very stubborn and strong headed young lady, getting her way whenever possible. Pris asked Henry if Mary had been well while they were in Savannah. Henry assured her Mary was in good health while they were away, "but on the way home on the boat she started having bad dreams and seeing this woman in black." Henry filled Pris in on the details while Sara hovered over Mary. Mathew came to the house around eight a.m. for breakfast and was surprised to find that everyone was up and Mary and Henry were back. Mary wanted to know about Luke.

He filled her in on all of his progress, "He handles the horses better than anyone we know. He moved out of the house to the cottage. He said it was too lonely without Mary around."

She wanted to see him, but was just too tired for now to find him. Sara went upstairs to ready the guest rooms for Mary's future in-laws arrival. Mary decided to take a nap while Henry went over to fetch them. Mary did not know Henry was going to tell his parents about her family history and what she was going through. She didn't want anyone to know she was ashamed of the fact she may be crazy.

She was having serious doubts about her forthcoming marriage. She could not put Henry through what her father lived through with her mother. She entered her room and wasn't surprised that it was cold, it was just a thing she accepted. She put on her dressing gown and lay across her bed. She fell into a deep, deep sleep.

Mary was being carried somewhere, she was so tired she just begged to be left alone to sleep. She could barely open her eyes, they were moving through what looked like a tunnel. Where was she being taken? She gave in to exhaustion once more.

When Mary awakened, she couldn't make out her surroundings. This was not her room. She sat up slowly and looked around. She was lying on a flat cold hard surface. She froze, she knew it was the altar.

CHAPTER TWENTY

Mary jumped up and ran, she didn't know where she was going and she just needed to get away. She was screaming, but there was no one to hear her. Luke was out riding when he heard a scream, he didn't know his beloved was back from her trip. He rode faster toward the screaming. He thought someone was hurt, but couldn't figure out who it could be. Luke found Mary stumbling around in the woods near the stream. He jumped from his horse and grabbed her up. She was in her night clothes and looked wild.

He was afraid for her, he had never seen anyone with such terror in their eyes. She could not speak a word. He picked her up and carried her to the house. Sara and Pris were under the impression she was upstairs asleep. No one left the house from downstairs. They both were there and would have known if Mary had come down. But she got out somehow.

Luke put Mary on the sofa. Sara brought a cool cloth and smelling salts. Pris sent Luke for Mathew so he could go across and get the doctor from the town, Mary needed more help than they could give her. The doctor arrived along with Henry, Mathew found him also. The doctor ordered a sedative and restraints for Mary until she calmed down.

Mary kept screaming, "He'll get me, don't tie me down please. Henry, don't let them do this." He could not bear to see her eyes plead with them and left the room.

Luke stayed and sat by her bed soothing her damp hair away from her forehead. "Luke, I'm not crazy I was sleeping. I woke up, but I was so tired. I was being carried through a tunnel, but I passed out again. When I woke up, I was on the altar at the middle of the island. I was terrified I just jumped up and ran. I don't remember anymore."

Luke told her that he was riding and heard someone screaming. "It was you Mary, you were terrified of something. I brought you home and the doctor was called. Henry came back with him. Everyone's afraid you'll hurt yourself or get hurt during these blackouts. I believe you Mary, and I swear I won't leave you."

Luke was not wise in the ways of the world, but he knew something was going on here far beyond Mary's hysterics. Someone was trying to scare this poor girl to death or drive her crazy. And he would find out who if it killed him. He sat guard at her bedside for several days with no incidents. Mary looked more like her old self. The restraints were removed and she was allowed out of bed for a few hours a day.

Sara was in constant attendance to Mary, as was Pris, but Henry's visits were short. It was as though he couldn't stand to look at her. He decided it was best to leave his parents at Pineda. He told his parents the whole story and though they were sympathetic, they encouraged Henry to break it off while he still could. Henry was pulled between Mary and his parents. He was afraid that all the stories were true, and he didn't want the mother of his children to end up like Mary's mother.

Henry began to just go off into another world himself, trying to figure out what to do. Luke was the solid foundation of support for Mary. Mary was distraught at Henry's behavior, but she understood. How could anyone love a person that just went off the deep end at times? She had Luke, Pris and Sara, but her heart ached for Henry. Luke watched all the people around Mary, he trusted no one. During every episode Mary experienced, no one was around except her. It was strange, things only happened when she was alone. Luke was going to be watching everyone, he just wouldn' t let them know he was watching. He wasn't sure about Mathew, but he knew Sara too well to believe she had anything to do with what was happening.

Even as much as Pris appeared to love and cherish Mary, he would watch her. He didn't know what else to do. Luke followed Pris around when she was unaware of his presence to see if she was staging any of these unexplainable events. So far she did nothing unusual, to his joy. Pris was in love with Mathew, but Mary was her only family. Mary owned everything, Mathew owned nothing. He was just a poor stable man. But to watch the two of them, they doted on her.

Luke was so confused. He would keep looking, there must be an explanation. Mary was more and more like her old self. Luke spent hours with her, letting Mathew take over the stables. He was devoted to her and would protect her from whomever or whatever was haunting her. He slept outside her room at night, to make sure no one entered. Henry was rarely around anymore. Everyone thought it was out of guilt for leaving Mary when she needed him. There was no more talk of marriage or plans for the future. Mary and Henry were polite to each other, not like people that were supposed to be in love.

Mary was the only person ever to love him and take care of him besides Barnamus. He wouldn't let her down. He moved around the house as if stalking prey. When he lived in the woods he learned the art of sneaking up on his prey.

Luke was outside Mary's room one night when he heard something across the hall. He knew the room was empty, but he got up to check on it. Upon entering the room, someone hit Luke over the head, knocking him out cold. That was the last he remembered for awhile. Luke did not know how long he was unconscious. He jumped up and ran to Mary's room. The door was open and Mary was gone. There was a large bump on his head.

CHAPTER TWENTY-ONE

Luke staggered back to the room across the hall and went inside. There was a door open to what looked like a closet. Luke went over and went inside. It was a secret staircase that went downstairs to the basement. He went downstairs and followed a passage leading out of the basement, it was apparent someone came into the house from outside. He followed the tunnel and ended up in the woods near a flat rock.

He looked around but found no trace of Mary. Luke needed to get some help. Upon returning to the house, he awoke Pris, Sara, and Mathew. He told them what happened. Pris passed out cold. He knew for certain Pris could not be behind what happened.

Mathew and Luke searched on into the night for Mary. They covered the stables, the cottage, the boat house, Mary's garden, and the cemetery but found nothing.

Pris was walking the floors, wringing her hands, mumbling, "If I hadn't come back to this horrible place, my Mary would be safe. Oh, why didn't I stop her?"

Luke had no idea what Pris was talking about. Luke was not aware of the stories of Mary's mother's insanity or the ghostly visits that Mary experienced while here. He was wondering if Pris wasn't loosing her mind.

Sara fixed coffee and rolls for everyone, but no one seemed to be hungry. Sara needed to keep busy. She was worried about her beloved Mary and now was concerned about Pris as well.

At dawn, Luke walked the tunnel again with a light, looking for some clues, but he found nothing. He went to the stables and saddled his horse and covered the island inch by inch. He thought he had covered the whole island, but there was a place he knew nothing about even though he lived here all his life. There was an old storm shelter about two hundred yards from the house that was forgotten over time, except by one person. Luke spent all day tracking and retracing his steps of the night before. His head hurt, he was tired and confused, but he couldn't give up.

About nine thirty that night, Mathew finally convinced Luke to get some rest. Luke went up and laid down on Mary's bed. At least he would feel close to her here. He drifted off to sleep and was running in the forest with his beloved friends again the ones he grew up with in the woods. He felt at peace in the wild.

He was startled out of a deep sleep by someone standing over his bed. A woman in a black dress was standing there crying. She motioned for him to follow her, he didn't know quite what to make of this. He arose and went with her. She went to the window and pointed across the yard and disappeared.

Luke saw nothing outside. He was truly very confused now. He went down and woke Mathew and told him what just took place. Mathew was pale by the time Luke finished his story.

He told Luke he had heard strange tales of this place, but didn't put any confidence in the stories. Luke wanted to know all about them so they were up the remainder of the night.

When Mathew finished with the story, Luke was astonished. They drank some coffee and started the search for a second day. Luke didn't know where else to look. He roamed the backyard that morning, wondering what the woman was trying to tell him when she pointed to the backyard. Luke decided to tell Pris, maybe she knew what it was all about.

When Luke told Pris, she told him to let her think about it for awhile. Pris was very young when this island was bought and there was a tremendous amount of remodeling done of the main house and grounds. She started looking immediately. She looked through her father's old desk, no one had disturbed any of its contents since his death.

Finally she came across some old drawings of the place. There appeared to be a lot of changes since the original owners sold it. There was a storm cellar at the back of the house, through the gate towards the woods. She'd never seen it though. She told Luke about this and he and Mathew went in search of a hidden door.

There was a stone wall covered with vines that circled the garden. They started looking for a door, feeling around on the wall. About half way down the south wall they found it. It was hidden. There was a rusty old lock on the door, so Luke went to get a sledge hammer to pound it off with. It took a while, but he and Mathew managed to knock the lock off.

They pulled the door open and entered a room. It appeared to have been lived in. They looked at each other in surprise. They lit a torch and what they saw was astonishing. There were all kinds of animal hides that were dried, food supplies, cooking utensils. Someone was living here.

They followed a tunnel, which seemed to be leading back toward the house, out of the room. About one hundred yards in, there was another room off to the side with a cot, and their lay Mary tied and gagged. Luke rushed to her, pulled her into his arms and held her before removing her ropes and gag.

She told Luke a man took her from the house and brought her here. "He's crazy, Luke. He kept mumbling to himself, 'I'm going to make you pay for what you have done.' Then he tied me up and left me alone. Please get me out of here." Luke and Mathew took her out the way they came in.

Pris and Sara were thrilled. They had found Mary and she was safe. Luke was positive the tunnel lead to somewhere within the house and he would return to see where, after he made sure Mary was safe. Luke told Pris to keep Mary downstairs in Sara's room with the door locked. Luke then returned to the storm cellar with Mathew. Pris wouldn't hear of Luke going alone.

"We retraced our tracks to the room where we found Mary then proceeded on down the tunnel. We were almost to the end when we saw a man approach.

"The intruder had seen us and took off back down the tunnel. We followed watching carefully for other rooms that might be hidden off to the side of the tunnel. The tunnel stopped in the basement. There was a door behind the wine rack that opened outward."

The basement was empty, that meant he was in the house. Luke and Mathew ran up the stairs to see about the women.

Pris and Sara were standing in the middle of the kitchen in shock. When Pris could finally speak, she told Luke and Mathew that she saw Charles come up out of the basement.

Mathew said, "I thought Charles was dead."

"That's what we were lead to believe when Mary received the letter from his estate. What has happened to my brother? Why would he kidnap his daughter?"

"We have to be careful he's in the house somewhere, there's no telling what he might do."

"Mary's locked in Sara's room for now. We'll watch her one on one. We will take shifts. Sara and I will sit with Mary, you and Luke watch the house."

The two men searched the entire house and didn't find Charles. How had he disappeared? Luke and Mathew needed to search every room, every wall to see if there were more hidden rooms. They could do better in the morning.

Luke took the first watch everybody moved downstairs so they wouldn't be spread out through the house. Luke listened for strange sounds through the night but heard nothing out of the ordinary.

Mary lay across Sara's bed wondering about this man who was her father. How many years had Charles been this way? What finally made him snap? Why did he blame her for what happened to Beth? She was grieved about her situation. Mary was here on the island with her dad and couldn't even get near him because he was insane. Charles wanted to hurt her.

Pris and Sara were sitting by her bed quietly. They both thought she was asleep. Mary couldn't be alone right now, she was in fear of being taken away and not being found. Everyone must leave this place and soon. But what about Charles?

Mathew was glad to see sunrise. It was hard to see the rooms by candlelight and lanterns. He and Luke would search again today for Charles. Mathew needed to send the women off the island to Pineda where they'd be safe.

The ladies fixed breakfast for everyone and the men went in search of Charles. Pris, Sara and Mary stayed locked in Sara's room off the kitchen.

"We retraced our tracks back down the tunnel. We saw this figure approaching.

"We quickly put out our light and waited. When he was close enough, we grabbed him and pinned him to the ground. The man was extremely strong, it's all we could do to handle him. It was as if we were fighting ten men instead of one.

"We finally managed to trap his arms and tied him up. He suddenly quit fighting us, as if the life had gone out of him. We led him on to the house through the tunnel, which came out in the basement. We took him upstairs. When we got in the light, we could see silver hair and a beard."

They went into the kitchen and called Sara and Pris.

Pris froze in her tracks, eyes piercing past them to the stranger. When she was able to speak, she called out with a heartbreaking cry. "Charles!"

CHAPTER TWENTY-TWO

Mathew put Charles in one of the bedrooms and locked the door. Surely he'd be safe there until something could be figured out. Mathew went back downstairs to talk to Pris.

"Pris, what do we do about Charles, he needs help. Should I fetch the doctor to sedate him? Luke would be here with you."

"Mathew let's see what happens, we'll let him calm down and then try to reach him. Maybe he'll recognize me. It's been a long time but just maybe something will spark a memory."

"Looks like he's got too many of those now."

"I know, Mathew, but I mean the good ones."

Charles was off in another world. He was rambling on and on about Beth and that he'd fix that brat that killed his Beth.

Pris couldn't believe what she was hearing. The years really were hard on him. And day by day his bitterness grew until there was so much hatred it consumed him. He planned to kill his own child. He felt that Mary would want to see where she was born so years previously he had devised a plan to get her here. Living alone for so long drove him mad. The only thing that kept him going was revenge.

Mary fell for the plot and arrived just as he believed she would. He only tried to scare her at first, but he lost control and revenge took over his mind and body. Mary couldn't believe it was her father. Not knowing her, how could he do this to her? She felt sorry for him, living alone and isolated all these years, growing old and bitter.

They could hear him pacing back and forth across the room. He was agitated for sure. Finally things quieted down. Maybe he's asleep.

Mathew and Luke would check, but they'd be cautious about it. He was very strong to be old. They opened the door cautiously and peeked in. Charles was gone.

"Now where did he go, these rooms have more secret doors and hallways than I've ever seen. Who would build such a house and why?"

Both went downstairs and told Pris Charles was gone. They were wasting time and energy looking for him. They had to get off the island.

Plans were underway to leave. In two days the boat would come over with supplies they would catch it and get back to the mainland, then get together some people come back and find Charles.

Surely they would be safe for two days. The horses needed to be fed and watered so the two men went together to take care of them.

Pris and Sara fixed the evening meal while the men were gone. Both doors were barred and they listened for the return of the men. Everyone's nerves were on edge.

How dangerous was Charles? They already knew he was capable of kidnapping. And he kept saying he was going to kill Mary.

They just didn't know how dangerous Charles really could be. He eluded the man-hunt always one step ahead. Charles was sure Barnamus was helping him. He was very delusional.

Charles was carrying on a conversation with Barnamus in his head. He promised Barnamus he would get revenge for his death.

"Barnamus there all around us closing in on all sides. I'll get them all, I'll trap them. I have to use myself for bait but I'll take care of everything don't worry. We'll never be misled again."

Charles watched from a distance as Luke and Mathew searched every corner of the cottage and stables. Charles had hidden the horses. He wouldn't give them the opportunity to ride away.

Next he had to catch that confounded person that kept coming over with the boat. He wanted to make sure there was no way off this island when he completed his plans for revenge.

Charles met the boat. The guy was pulling into the dock and yelled up at Charles to grab the rope. Charles grabbed and tied off the end. "How goes it?" Charles didn't answer. The man thought him very odd.

The fisherman climbed off the boat to finish tying the rope and turned to catch the stern when everything went black. Charles had hit him over the head. Before he could come to, Charles climbed on the boat and pushed off. He would take it out a ways and sink it. He could swim back to shore.

"The fisherman sat up rubbing his head. What happened? Where's my boat?"

Luke and Mathew came running down to the dock to see what was up. Where was the boat?

The fisherman told them some guy met him and next thing he knew, he was picking himself up off the ground and his boat was gone. Who was that maniac?"

"We assume it was Charles Windsor. We found him living here a few days ago. There's a lot that's happened here since Mary came to live here. We'll fill you in on the way to the house. Everyone thought he was dead. But he is here and clearly has lost his mind." They helped him to the house. His head hurt. Charles must have hit him with a club.

Pris was in the kitchen when the three walked in the back door. "What's happened Luke?"

"Charles hit him over the head and took the boat."

"Oh no. Now what are we going to do? We're stranded here now. What's Charles up to? Sara we're in trouble. Mary is my priority I'll protect her with my life. He's my brother, but Mary comes first. He left us over eighteen years ago. Mary is my daughter now."

How are we going to bar the house where he can't get in? He knows all about the secret passages."

Mary felt guilty for putting them all in danger. She was the reason they were trapped here. If she'd listened to Pris they wouldn't be here. How could she get them out of this? She needed to think.

She was the one Charles wanted, maybe she should go to him and try to reason with him. How did you reason with someone that wasn't living in the real world?

Mary could hear the others talking in the kitchen. There were six of them, to one of him. Luke was the only one beside Charles that knew the island well. Maybe he could figure out where Charles was hiding.

Charles went off shore a short distance. He went down in the hull and pulled the plug. Water started pouring in, filling up the lower bowels of the boat fast. Charles got back up top and jumped overboard. He let the current carry him to shore. Now to put his plan in action. He would eliminate them one by one until he was the only one left.

Charles entered the house around midnight. He would make sure they knew he was there. He was in the upstairs bedroom slamming doors. He'd wake the whole house if they were sleeping.

Luke and Mathew headed for the stairs. "Wait Luke, maybe he wants us to separate. That may be his plan to conquer us."

Pris told Luke the fisherman might have a point there. “He’s got something in mind or he wouldn’t let us know he was here.”

CHAPTER TWENTY-THREE

Mary was dreaming she was being chased by her father, but it wasn't her father. The dream was very confusing. Where was she? She didn't recognize her surroundings. Who was the woman floating toward her in black? Pris, where are you? I'm scared.

Mary could tell the woman was young, she had a slender build of a young girl. Why was she dressed so horridly? As the girl floated by Mary saw herself in mourning clothes. What was going on? Who was dead?

Mary walked on down the hall looking around trying to get her bearings. She knew these rooms, she'd played here as a child. Oh, where was Pris? Mary kept calling and calling but Pris wouldn't answer.

Mary entered one of the many rooms and walked slowly up to the bed. Someone was lying there so still. Who could it be? As she crept closer and closer her heart was racing. As she feared it was Pris. Mary screamed and screamed. No, Pris, don't leave me you have to protect me from that monster who thinks he's my father, come back Pris, don't leave me alone.

Mary fell down by the bed weeping. Now she was truly alone. No mother, father or aunt to care for her. What would she do? She knew nothing about caring for herself. She always depended on Pris to make the right decisions about her life. How would she live? She knew nothing of finances, she knew they had money but not how much or even where it was kept.

Mary needed to get up and run. She was in terrible danger, someone was coming and she needed to hide. Mary went to the closet and stepped in. In through the door walked her father. Charles looked around as if he knew she was there but he'd play her game for awhile. Charles looked down at Pris threw his head back and laughed and left the room.

Mary thought how horrid to do that to your own sister. She wondered where Luke, Mathew and Sara were. Oh, where is everybody? Mary was so scared she didn't know what to do but she knew she must not stay here Charles would be back.

Mary slipped out of the closet and looked out the door into the hall. When she felt it was safe she went into the hall and headed for the stairs. She would get out of this house. She'd have more room outside to hide than in here. Mary was in the parlor when she heard a noise, she froze. She could hear someone moving about in the kitchen. She wondered if it could be Sara.

Mary was too afraid to find out so she went running out the door in a big hurry. She was almost to the garden before she slowed down. It dawned on her she needed to slow down and be careful. She didn't want to get reckless and get herself caught.

Mary checked out the garden before she went in. No sign of anyone yet. Was she alone here, had everyone left her? Pris was dead so she couldn't protect her, but where were the others? Mary wanted to sit and think but instincts told her to keep moving. I have to get out of the open, I must hide.

Just then Charles appeared in the garden with Mary. I've finally got you where I want you. Now you will pay for killing my Beth. Mary took off in a run. She would not let him catch her, she couldn't, he was going to kill her.

Mary headed for the lighthouse. She didn't have any idea where she would hide she was just running blind. Someone needed to help her and soon. She could hear the waves pounding on shore, the ocean was getting rough. Mary thought about swimming around the cove and finding a hiding place.

Where could Luke's hiding place be? She knew he hid from people for years and wasn't found, so where was it. Mary knew she needed to find it and quick. She ran toward the cliff . She couldn't wind up trapping herself with Charles on her heels.

Mary lay down at the edge and looked over. There on the side of the cliff was an opening. She carefully lowered herself down to a ledge and slipped inside. It was a cave. So this is where Luke hides from the world. It was out of sight and it was perfect for keeping dry during the raging storms they got here on the coast. Mary wondered if Charles knew of this place. She'd have to take her chance, she was alone and in need of a rest.

Mary sat for awhile listening to the ocean below. Just then a figure filled the opening. She strained her eyes to make out the presence. It was Barnamus standing there looking at her. He stretched out his hand to her and disappeared. Mary awoke with a start. She jumped up and ran in the kitchen where Pris and Sara were fixing the evening meal.

Pris could see the fright on Mary's face. She went to her and put her arms around her and held her close. Mary I'm so sorry for what has happened here. My brother is trying to kill his own daughter, because he doesn't know what he's doing. Now we're all his prisoners.

"Pris, I had a horrible dream. You were dead and everyone else was gone. I was here with my father alone and he was chasing me. I got outside and ran toward the lighthouse. Not knowing for sure where I was going. But I looked over the bank where Maria fell and there was a ledge below. I climbed down and it was hiding a cave. That's where Luke has been hiding all these years.

"I went inside and looked around and someone entered the mouth of the cave. I strained my eyes to see and I saw Barnamus. He stretched out his hand to me and disappeared. That's when I woke up.

"What is he trying to tell me? He's trying to protect me, but I don't know how yet. Pris, I'm frightened. How can we reach my father? I know in my heart he doesn't really want to hurt me. It's whatever evil has taken over his mind. Do you think we can reach him somehow Pris?"

"I don't know Mary, he's upstairs now that's what all the noise is. He wants us to know he's here. We don't know what he's up to yet. We're afraid to separate to find out, that may be his plan. I guess we just wait it out for the night. Maybe we can come up with something soon. I guess we're confined to these two rooms for now.

"We'll take turns sleeping. Two will be awake at all times. It will be safer that way. We'll just keep the coffee pot going." Mathew and Luke took the first watch. The captain and one of the ladies would take the second watch. It would be a long night.

Nobody got any sleep that night even knowing Mathew and Luke were on watch. Charles was in the house somewhere and they felt like sitting ducks. He could be in the next room for all they knew. Mary was wondering how they were going to get out of this. Would anyone miss the captain when he didn't return and come looking?

He was not very popular because of his sarcasm. It's like he had a big chip on his shoulder and was looking for a fight at any time. Mary felt sorry for him. What could have made him so angry?

Captain Nathaniel McCormick had lived in Pineda for near fifty years. He remembered well the day he sailed into the cove at Pineda.

He was tying his boat to the dock when he saw her. He couldn't take his eyes off this beautiful southern belle.

Nathaniel knew he had to make her acquaintance. Their eyes met and held. She smiled and walked up the dock with a backward glance. Nathaniel's heart stood still. He would make inquiries to try to find out more about the lady that had captured his heart.

Lydia Goodman was her name; she lived on the coast of Pineda. Her father was a very wealthy businessman. He transported fruits from the orange groves to different parts of the world. Lydia lived near the beach. She could see the ocean from her bedroom windows. Lydia loved the ocean and enjoyed long walks on the beach in the cool of the evening.

Nathaniel found this information very helpful. He would make sure he was on the beach that afternoon and introduce himself to her. Nathaniel got his boat docked and set out to get some much needed supplies. Nathaniel had been off shore for weeks and he needed everything. After that Nathaniel would find accommodations for a hot bath.

Nathaniel was finished his chores by four in the evening and settled down to wait for Lydia on the beach. He loved the sound of the waves pounding the shore. To live on a boat was a dream come true to him. He had left New York and his family to cruise down the east coast. It had taken months and a few bad storms on the way to get here. But here he was waiting on the beach for a girl that all he knew about her was her name.

Lydia walked the beach in thought. This was her time to get away from reality.

Since her mother died it was a constant struggle to get anything done. She missed her so much. And her poor father was beside himself. Mr. Goodman worked harder than ever. Lydia knew it was from grief. Lydia was aware every time he looked at her he saw Jolene. Lydia came to the beach for comfort. It was her mother's favorite place too.

CHAPTER TWENTY-FOUR

Lydia was strolling mindlessly along when she noticed the young man from the boat. She smiled and said hello to him. Nathaniel introduced himself to Lydia and asked if he could stroll along with her. Lydia welcomed his company. She also wanted to get to know the handsome young stranger.

Nathaniel stayed in port for weeks getting to know Lydia. He longed to be with her more and more. Nathaniel approached Mr. Goodman about a job. Mr. Goodman put him to work supervising the loading of the ships. Nathaniel was a very happy man. He intended to ask Lydia for her hand in marriage.

He first wanted to get settled and buy a home for her so she would have a place to come to as his bride. They were married in June. It was a lovely ceremony and the reception was grand. Mr. Goodman had gone all out with the party. Nathaniel and Lydia went to there new home after everyone left and so began their life together.

Nathaniel was a very proud man. He was successful in his work had a beautiful wife and was soon to be proud father. Lydia was due in the fall. She was radiant during her pregnancies. Lydia gave birth to a girl and a boy. The baby girl grew and was a delight to both parents. The baby boy lived three days and died. Nathaniel was heart broken.

He wanted a son to follow in his footsteps. Lydia was unable to bear more children. That made their daughter even more precious to them. Nathaniel and Lydia watched as Catherine grew into a lovely young woman. Catherine met this no good lazy drifter and wanted to get married. Catherine's parents forbade this. So one stormy night they eloped. The whole town knew she was missing, but they would rather believe that it was Barnamus doing. Instead of checking things out the crowd got out of control and went to the island. When they got there they found Barnamus. Nathaniel lived a life of grief and sorrow for what they did to an innocent man.

Nathaniel grew cold and bitter looking for fights anywhere he could find one. Lydia died from grief. After Lydia died he began running his little boat again. He found enough customers to keep him busy. At least he didn't have to think. So this was the life of Captain Nathaniel McCormick.

Nathaniel wondered how they were going to get out of this mess. His boat was gone, he was on an island he hated with a mad man. Nathaniel knew nobody would miss him for days. He was accustomed to just disappearing for days at a time. Surely they could come up with a way to capture Charles.

Mathew's thoughts were along the same line as Nathaniel's. Someone had to come up with a plan to capture this man before he hurt someone seriously, or killed someone instead. Mathew would talk to Luke and Nathaneil later when the ladies were busy fixing breakfast.

Luke thought about a plan of action to help with knowing where Charles was. They could set small traps up to see how many he went through around the house. They would check them hourly. They would keep looking until they found all of the secret hiding places in the house.

Luke, Mathew and Nathaneil went to work checking the house out. They put flour down on the floor in the dark passages of the house. This way they could tell if he'd been in the passage way. They couldn't believe all the hiding places that were built into the house. After much work they returned to the kitchen for a rest and something to drink.

Mary asked how the search turned out. "Mary there are all kind of passages through out the house. No wonder we've not been able to catch him. He has used these for years and knows what he's doing. It might be very hard to catch him. But we will do our best."

They knew there was no way off this island. All they could do now was try to survive. Mary hated being closed inside like this, she was getting restless. But did she dare venture outside? If she could just swim in the cool water of the ocean. Mary asked Mathew if it were possible to go for a swim.

Mathew told her he would take her to the beach for a swim later. "Luke and I will escort you there and back. We know it is hard on all of us being locked in like this. We just have to be careful."

Mary thought it would be nice if Henry would come and check on them. Since their breakup she had not heard from him. He really thought she was crazy. She could not blame him it did appear to be true. But with all the current events of her father being alive and hunting her, she could prove she was not mad.

But would she want a man that had abandoned her in her hour of need. What kind of husband would he have made? Mary tried hard not to think of all this now. Her main priority was keeping Pris and the others safe.

Mary felt sorry for her father, but he abandoned her a long time ago. Her parent was Pris. Mary couldn't wait to get off this island. If and when this happened she'd never come back here again.

Mary made up her mind not to hide from Charles. She would bait him out into the opening. Then the men could over power him. She would talk to Mathew about it. She knew she couldn't tell Pris it would worry her too much. Mary pulled Mathew aside and told him of the plan.

Mathew thought she was right. Charles wanted Mary and that's what they'd have to use to leer him out. The only question was where would it be safe enough to do this? Mathew thought of the cabin. They could surround it, put Mary inside and watch for Charles.

Mathew knew all three could overtake Charles. They could chain him in the cabin like they had chained Luke. It had to work. Mary told Pris they were going for a swim. "Mathew and Nathaneil will be with me and Luke will be with you."

Pris wouldn't hear of Luke staying with them. "We are locked in this house and we're safe. There are no secret passages to this part of the house. And we will not unlock the door. I understand the need to get out. Go enjoy yourself as much as you can. I'm sorry, my dear, I let you come here."

"Pris, it wasn't your fault. I was strong willed and wanted to see where I was born. Don't blame yourself please." Pris was so taken with Mary's maturity. Pris raised Mary well.

Mary, Mathew, Luke and Nathaneil left for the beach. As they got on the pathway the men ducked into the woods. Mary walked on to the beach. She tried to act as if nothing out of the ordinary was happening. She glanced around causally. Mary waded in the edge of the water. It felt good on her feet. She disrobed down to her swim suit and dove in.

The water was wonderful. She swam and let her mind drift back to happier days before all this. Mary remembered her holidays with family. The visits from cousins from Savannah. The merriment when they were at her home. The Christmas carols they sang in the neighborhood. The meals that were shared between them.

Mary's heart was breaking into a million pieces. She was crying for the love of a father she never knew. And now that man was trying to kill her. Mary cried for her mother who never got to love and raise her own daughter.

Mary was exhausted by the time she rid herself of the frustration of events taking place here. She didn't think she could cry anymore. Mary came out of the water and dressed. She would head to the cabin now. What ever happened she had lived a good life with Pris. Mary just hoped the men got to her in time.

Mary entered the cabin and sat down on the bed they moved from the house for Luke. That seemed like an eternity ago. Mary knew she was safe because the men were outside watching the cabin. Still she felt this growing uneasiness in the pit of her stomach. Mary was so tired she fell asleep sitting up. She didn't know how long she dozed before being awakened by a noise.

Beth stood before her daughter crying. "Mother, why are you crying? I am safe my friends are outside to protect me."

Beth told Mary that she was not safe and wouldn't be until Charles was dead. "He is a mad man out for revenge for something you didn't do. My dear, there is much sorrow ahead for you. I will be near. I will protect you as much as I can. Please be careful." Beth vanished.

Mary was not so sure this was a good idea anymore. Charles could overpower her friends. Then no one could protect her from him. Mary got up and walked around the room. Why did this have to be? Mary wished she'd never been born. Then Beth would be alive and Charles wouldn't be insane. She was to blame. Mary was endangering all the people she loved just by being here.

Mary looked around before climbing out the window. She would not stay and let Charles hurt her family. Mary quietly slipped away from the cabin. The only thing she knew to do was to let Charles know she was no longer with the others so he'd leave them alone.

Mary walked down the path to the cliffs watching over her shoulder. She would hide in the cave below the cliff. Mary hated doing this to Pris but keeping her aunt safe was more important.

Mary saw Charles before he saw her. Mary was a good runner. She knew she could out run him. He was old and slightly bent. Mary called out to him. "Charles."

Charles turned and looked at Mary. Charles thought it was Beth. "Beth, where have you been I was so worried. You need to stay closer to the house dear. The cliffs are dangerous."

Mary told Charles "I'm not Beth. I'm Mary, your daughter."

Charles screamed in agony "No". Mary turned and ran. Now he knew she was no longer with the others. He would leave them alone and pursue her.

Mary would sneak back to the house later for food and water. She was so hungry. Mary knew everyone was looking for her. She just needed to be elusive for now. She didn't need to get caught. Her plans would be ruined.

Mathew, Luke and Nathaniel watched the cabin. They were not aware that Mary was gone. It was getting late so they decided to get Mary and head home for a meal. All three entered the cabin to find it empty. "How could this be we were just outside." Luke and Nathaniel looked bewildered. What would they tell Pris and Sara? They needed to find Mary and fast.

Mathew hated telling Pris that Mary was missing. The men discussed how to go about finding her. Nathaneil and Luke would begin the search while Mathew went to break the news to Pris and Sara.

Pris was at the stove when Mathew entered alone. Pris could tell something was not right. Mathew came over to Pris put his arm around her and told her what happened at the cabin. "Pris, I'm so sorry. Mary wanted to catch him before he hurt one of us. She feels responsible for us being here and in danger.

"We were watching the cabin, the only way out was the window. We figured if he came in she would scream. We heard nothing. Nathaniel and Luke are searching for her now. I'll grab them something to eat and rejoin them in the search. Unless you'd rather I stay with you and Sara."

"No, we're fine, just find Mary for me, please."

Mathew grabbed some food and water and headed out the door. This was going to be a long night.

Mary ran and ran. She knew she had lost Charles it was just good to run off some of her energy. Mary found the cave and entered. It was dark inside. She would wait until her eyes adjust. Then she would be able to see. The cave was exactly like what she remembered from her dream.

How did she know these things? Mary had never experienced this type of knowledge before. What was it about being on Singer Island that changed things. Mary looked like the young lady that came to marry Barnamus. Then there was her mother. Some great force was protecting her, she was sure of it. Mary hadn't thought much about spirits or ghosts, if that's what you wanted to call them. She knew now for sure there was something beyond death. She was just thankful she had guardians watching over her.

Pris and Sara were walking the floor worried out of their minds. Where could their precious Mary be? What had happened to her? How did Charles get her out of the cabin? All they could do was pray for Mary's safety.

Mathew caught up with Luke and Nathaneil. After eating and resting for awhile they continued to search for Mary. They had no idea Mary went off on her own. They were sure Charles was responsible for her disappearance.

Luke wanted to check the cave below the cliff. He knew Mary was aware of its existence. They talked about it several times while he was at the cabin hidden. Maybe she would be there. Luke didn't know if Charles knew about the cave or not. It wouldn't hurt to look.

They took off in the direction of the cliff. As they neared they could hear the ocean. How familiar this was to Luke. After all this was where he had lived all his life. Luke volunteered to go down the path to the cave. The path was worn with years of use from Luke. As he approached the cave he heard something inside.

Mary saw the opening of the cave darken. Her pulse was racing. She never thought of what to do if Charles found her. Well, she'd do what she needed to do to survive.

Luke whispered, "Mary are you in there?" Mary answered when she realized it was her friend Luke. She ran and put her arms around Luke. "Mary what are you doing here? Where's Charles? How did he get you out of the cabin?"

"Luke, he didn't I climbed out the window. I've put everyone in danger. I thought if I got alone I could draw him out. That way he wouldn't bother the rest of you. I couldn't stand thinking one of you could get hurt because of me."

"Mary, you're not to blame. Now lets get you home. Pris and Sara are going out of their minds not knowing where you are."

Luke and Mary climbed up the cliff to where Mathew and Nathaniel were waiting. Charles was watching them from near by.

How did they find her so quickly? Charles suspected she was in the cave. But he was waiting until it got dark. Charles planned to go in and surprise her. That way she couldn't escape. He would be blocking the only way in and out. But now she was back with the others. Well, he'd make them all pay for robbing him of his victory.

Mathew and Nathaneil were never so happy to see anybody in their lives. When Mary stepped up on the bank of the cliff. Luke was right, she did go to the cave.

Mary explained to them why she left the cabin. She apologized for worrying them all. Mary was eager to get to Pris. Mary knew Pris would be pacing the floor. She knew she would hear a lecture, but that was alright. Mary deserved it. She knew better than to take off. She just didn't want her family hurt.

CHAPTER TWENTY-FIVE

Charles got to the house and entered. He went upstairs to one of the bedrooms. He would be rid of all these people tonight. He had a plan.

Mary entered the kitchen and ran to Priscilla's waiting arms. Pris rocked her back and forth while fussing at her for leaving the men's safety. Mary told Pris she was sorry. "I just couldn't stand being afraid anymore. I didn't know what might happen." Sara hugged Mary and started preparing food for everyone. She knew they were hungry. Sara fixed peas, corn, fried chicken and sweet potato pie. Everyone sat down to eat. They hadn't realized how hungry they were. Not a morsel was left from the meal. After the meal Luke suggested they all put there heads together and come up with a plan to catch Charles.

Priscilla still found it hard to believe he was alive. The brother she knew nineteen years ago was gone. This was a maniac. Someone driven by evil. To want to kill his own flesh and blood. It sickened her. She was glad Beth was not here to see her beloved Charles like this.

While they were talking Mary said "I smell smoke. Pris something's burning. Do you smell it?"

All at once smoke started seeping in under the door into the kitchen. The ladies screamed. Mathew took hold of Mary, Pris and Sara and led them toward the back door. It was locked from the other side. Charles had locked them in.

Nathaniel tried the door that led into the dinning room. "It's open. We'll have to make our way out the front. Stay low so you'll be below the smoke. Mathew and I will lead the ladies out. Luke you stay close."

The flames were hot. The smoke was thick and choking. They covered their mouth and noses but still could not filter out all the smoke. You couldn't see your hand in front of your face.

Mary just knew they were going to die. How horrid. Where was Luke? Mary still held on to Nathaniel's hand. Sara was right behind her. Would they never get out of this house?

Mary could hear the ceiling crashing down somewhere close by. Why couldn't they find the door? Mathew found the door but it was locked as well. He had no other choice but to break out a window. He needed to get the ladies to safety. Once he opened the window the fire would burn faster. Mathew had no choice.

Mathew grabbed a heavy chair and hurled it through the window. He pushed Mary outside first. Nathaniel was helping Sara out. Where were Luke and Pris? Mathew heard a scream and went back to the area where it seemed to be coming from. Mathew saw Charles choking Pris.

Mathew rammed his body into Charles which loosened his hold on Pris. Luke came up behind Charles and grabbed him around the waist. Mathew got Pris to the window and shoved her outside. He then tried to return to help Luke but the flames were wild. He couldn't see them anymore.

Mathew heard these awful screams. There was no way he could help Luke. Mathew jumped out the window with his coat on fire. Nathaniel grabbed and rolled him on the ground. Mary ran up screaming, "Where's Luke?" Mathew told her he couldn't get back through the fire to help him. Mary tried to pull away to go back in the house. But Nathaniel held on to her tightly.

Mary kept screaming Luke's name over and over. The house was ablaze the fire was so hot they were forced to back way off. All you could see was fire. "Dear Luke." He died to save us all from my father.

Mary would miss him terribly. She had looked forward to spending many years with Luke. Why, why did Charles have to do this?

Charles lost his own life and took Mary's best friend with him. They watched the house burn in disbelief. It was a miracle how they escaped with their lives. Charles didn't intend for anyone to leave that house alive. He nailed doors and windows shut to keep them inside. He used oil to set the fire. And the house, being as old as it was, the wood was old and dry. Which made it burn faster.

Everyone was exhausted, dirty and in shock. The house was gone along with their clothes and most of their food. Mathew and Nathaniel took the ladies to the cabin. At least they could rest there. The air was still thick with smoke. After getting Priscilla and Mary settled down, Sara fixed tea for everyone. Mathew kept a few provisions at the cabin. He used these when he stayed near the horses instead of going to the house.

Mathew and Nathaniel were going back to check the house and get whatever food was left from the smoke house out back. At least now everyone was safe. There was no way Charles made it out of the fire. And neither had Luke.

It was a very sad day. A friend and a brother were lost. Mathew and Nathaneil would search through the rubble when it cooled down.

Their biggest problem was getting off the island back to Pineda. Hopefully someone saw the fire and would come to investigate.

It didn't take them long to gather up the remainder of the food supply. A couple of smoked hams, potatoes, some bacon and a bag of flour. That would get them by for a few days.

Both men would need some sleep. They were exhausted. It was one of those days that seemed like it would never end.

Mary was asleep when they returned. Pris and Sara were sitting quietly. They both lost a friend. One they would miss. Pris lost a brother for the second time. But this time it was permanent. She almost lost Mary in the process. From now on she would be more protective of her niece. It seemed as if they were doomed. This island was nothing but bad news for anyone who owned it. Pris hoped when they left it would become wilderness again. Nobody needed to live here. Too many sad events happened here.

Pris would be glad when morning came. Mathew and Nathaneil planned to go back to the house as soon as it got light. Nobody really slept that night. When they closed their eyes they could see the fire. And the screams from Luke and Charles were heart rendering. It would haunt them for the rest of their lives.

Mathew and Nathaniel left the cabin at first light. They needed to check the ruins. Just to make sure Charles and Luke's body were there. They needed to bury them. Both men were in the middle of the house side by side. Their bodies were burned beyond recognition. It would be a gruesome job burying them.

It would take a strong stomach to handle them. But it must be done. Mathew and Nathaniel pulled the bodies out of the rubble. They made a stretcher out of a tarp and carried them to the cemetery. They would bury Charles by his wife, Beth. Luke would be buried by Barnamus.

It took all morning to dig the graves. They went ahead and buried them. The ladies didn't need to see them like this. Mathew would tell

Pris where Charles was buried. He knew they would hold a small service for them to pay their respects.

Mathew and Nathaniel went to the cabin to let the ladies know what they done. Pris, Mary and Sara were very sad. They missed Luke. They cleaned up best they could to go pay there last respects to Luke and Charles.

As they were going down the path to the cemetery they met a man by the name of Benjamin. He told them he saw the fire in Pineda. "People were worried so they asked me to come over and check on you."

"Mathew filled Benjamin in on what had happened. We're on our way to pay our respects to them. Then, if you would be so kind as to give us a ride back to Pineda we would be grateful."

Benjamin told them he would be glad to take them over. He would meet them at the dock. "Take your time. I'm in no hurry." Mary was weeping quietly for her friend. She was sad for her father too. But she didn't know him as she knew Luke. Everyone said their goodbyes and headed for the boat.

It was a relieve to be leaving this place. It held such a haunting atmosphere. Mary wanted to get back to being normal.

Mary wanted to go home. She knew she could never live on Singer Island again. It was never a happy place for anyone. It was only fitting to leave it. It would not be sold. Just forgotten like the sands of time. Eventually she would put all this behind her and live a normal life. But she would never forget Luke.

They walked down to the dock and got aboard Benjamin's boat. She would make arrangements for the horses to be moved. It was the last day on the Island and Mary was glad to be leaving. As the boat pulled away Mary took one last look. "Goodbye Luke I'll miss you."

THE END

ABOUT THE AUTHOR

Wanda James is a retired nurse. She grew up in the Golden Isles of South East Georgia. She roamed the islands as a child and grew to love their alluring mystical qualities. As an adult she worked on St. Simons at a retirement village. She met the famous writer Eugenia Price there while she was visiting a friend. Ms. Price was a great influence on Wanda, as was her grandmother, who wove tales of mystery and adventure. Wanda James moved to Upstate South Carolina, where she now lives with her husband and boxer puppy. Wanda's husband is also a nurse. They met while working at a Veterans Nursing Home and married in October 1998.

www.ingramcontent.com/pod-product-compliance
Ingram Content Group UK Ltd.
Pitfield, Milton Keynes, MK11 3LW, UK
UKHW041940190726
13854UKWH00004B/1702